THE NEW BIZARRO AUTHOR SERIES

PRESENTS

S.T. CARTLEDGE

Eraserhead Press
Portland, OR

THE NEW BIZARRO AUTHOR SERIES
An Imprint of Eraserhead Press

ERASERHEAD PRESS
205 NE BRYANT
PORTLAND, OR 97211

WWW.ERASERHEADPRESS.COM

ISBN: 1-62105-068-8

EDITOR'S NOTE

Remember that TV show, *House Hunter*, where some debutante would take a new couple around the city looking for their first home? Shane didn't even have to pitch this book including that TV show. It just came to mind and was immediately trounced by visions of what bizarro could do to it. And that's just what this is. This book is about wild houses running around doing house things, and the Lara Croft-type house hunter who trains them to be homes. And their crazy-ass journeys, of course.

S.T. Cartledge is a young Australian writer who is on his way into bizarro with shining weirdness. He's a bit like the protagonist in his story—finding the future by accepting what's thrown at him, seeking guidance, and taking advice easily, while maintaining his own character, skill, and charm. I think Shane's imagination will take him far. Let it take you now into his weird world of house-fights and other adventures. You might never look at houses the same.

I'm happy to present S.T. Cartledge's book as part of the New Bizarro Author Series. The NBAS strives to bring new voices in bizarro fiction to our readers. It serves as an opportunity to introduce you to new writers, and introduce them into the world of being an author. Eraserhead Press is happy to bring new, weird voices to you in the hopes that these authors will prove themselves to be strong members of the bizarro community and continue to entertain you for years to come. The publishing of this book marks the beginning of a one year proving period. Please help support our NBAS writers in their endeavors by telling your friends about their cool new books. The book you hold is only one of several hundred that must be sold in order for this author to continue on his path. We hope you help him along as best as you can. Thank you.

~~Kevin Shamel

AUTHOR'S NOTE

I would like to thank the writers who have supported me and offered criticism and words of encouragement. I would also like to thank my friends and family for believing in me and showing an interest in my work. I didn't write House Hunter for any specific person or people. I just wanted to entertain. At times I wanted to make you feel a little uneasy, and at other times I wanted to make you think. I enjoyed writing this book, as I hope you enjoy reading it.

1
FUNNEL WEB FARM

Three pigs were flattened by a house and there was not a wolf in sight. Imogen got a phone call at three in the morning. Mary Nolan couldn't stop blubbering and sobbing, her voice was so wet Imogen wanted to hand a tissue through the phone.

"H-h-house st-stomped on my pigs. Help!" Mary said.

Imogen climbed into her leather hunter jumpsuit, zipped up and pulled the straps tight. She checked her pockets, pouches and clips to make sure everything was in its right place; gloves, hooks, ropes, knife, lightning cannon. In her backpack; maps, tins of food, tin opener, portable stove, basic sanitary supplies, first-aid-kit, flashlight, safety harness, matches, and this weapon Imogen made herself—a bat with nails sticking through it. Clipped to the inside of the backpack were her origami spider walker and dragonfly transport creatures.

The house hunter scrunched her electric-blue hair into a little ponytail with a black hair-tie. She grabbed her goggles from a hook by the door and slipped them over her blue eyes.

Outside, she unfolded her spider walker, put her gloves on over her cold hands, and locked the house with a flick of her wrist. The backpack hugged her shoulders and the origami dragonfly breathed, expanding and contracting, massaging her back. She sat down on her spider walker and slotted her hands into the control sockets, merging with the machine. Imogen's face was white with a pale hexagonal pattern etched into her skin like a tattoo. The design ran down her neck and over her shoulders, she was nearly camouflaged when riding her spider shirtless—but that was only for fun, not work.

The walker, a white model with a blue head, ran through her front garden—roots, grass, and weeds tried to trip it up. The overhanging branches of trees whipped at Imogen's head. Somewhere beneath all that was the long gravel path that lead out to the neighborhood.

On the road, the spider walker picked up speed. The wind whipped through Imogen's hair, ran along the length of her body and dropped off her tail, leaving a vortex of dust in her wake. Her thighs squeezed against the spider walker as the chill wind permeated her jumpsuit. The spider's legs pumped hard, tilting over as it ripped around the corner.

A few streets over, the heavy footsteps of a house on the move shook the ground. It was big, slow and heavy. Each step it took boomed and and echoed. The sound became louder and sharper as Imogen approached the street.

It was an old Victorian house with four big claw feet, like the feet from an old, cast-iron bathtub. It stopped in the middle of the street.

Imogen brought her walker to a stop, and for a moment there was total silence in the neighborhood. The house seemed lost and confused—as many of these night-walking houses are—and Imogen wanted to help it. Her instinct was to take the house back to its home and train it proper, but she couldn't leave poor, blubbering Mary Nolan waiting. The spider walker side-stepped away from the great, classic beast. When she turned onto the highway, the echoes of the night-walker began again.

Coming up the driveway to Funnel Web Farm, Imogen's nostrils stung with the stench of dead swine. She hopped off the spider walker in the Nolans' front yard and slipped her goggles down around her neck.

Mary stood on the front porch, leaning on the railing for support—her black hair tied up in dozens of tight coils. "Th-thank you!" She said. Her eyes were silver with a thin green slit and they shuttered like a camera lens. "Keith has been trying to k-keep it under c-control until you got here." Her ridged skin rippled in the moonlight. "Is that th-thing all right in the front yard?" Mary pointed at the spider walker nuzzling its head in the garden.

"It'll be fine. It seems quite fond of your roses."

"Oh, yes . . . I suppose it does . . . Come with me."

Imogen followed Mary around the side of the house and across a paddock of funnel web ponies. They stopped at the gate to a paddock with a big acorn tree and a two-story farm house behind it, standing about a foot off the ground on hundreds of matchstick legs.

Keith Nolan was in the acorn tree, sitting on a low limb, an axe in one hand slung over his shoulder, and a gas filter mask on his face. Keith's head was long and white and bald like a snake egg, and his pink eyes stared at the house that was feasting on his pigs.

Imogen pulled a rag from her back pocket and tied it bandanna-style over her mouth and nose. She jumped the fence then ran up to the acorn tree, using her balance and momentum to kick off the base of the trunk and pull herself onto one of the lower branches. She climbed across a couple of branches, sat down across from Keith, and gave a friendly wave.

Signalling at his axe, Imogen said, "Can I borrow that?"

Keith passed it across and Imogen swung it over her head into the tree trunk. She used the axe head as a step up to the higher branches, getting closer to the first-story roof. The branches dipped and swayed beneath her weight as she climbed away from the trunk and held the other branches for support. She steadied her feet on a branch hanging over the house's rain gutter and leapt onto the roof, slipping on the roof tiles.

There were half a dozen pig carcasses at the front of the house where its legs had picked the pigs to shreds.

Imogen lowered her center of gravity, resting a palm on the roof. She gripped the gutter and swung down onto the porch, where she unstrapped her lightning cannon from her belt and clipped it to her forearm. The trigger was looped through her fingers, linked into her glove. Imogen turned the switch to *stun* and it hummed into life.

"Keith!" she yelled, "you'd better get out of the tree and back off a bit. She's in a fragile state. Not sure how she might react."

"Okay," he said.

The house's legs were slicked red with gore and blood at the edge of the porch, as it dismantled the pigs. Blood splashed up the steps to the front door. Bits of bone and flesh clung to the bottom step.

Imogen flicked her wrist and small sparks shot from her lightning cannon. The house recoiled and shivered, but continued smashing and slurping the pigs. Imogen knelt at the stairs and knocked on the top step. She paused, then knocked again.

The old farm house leapt and quivered. Imogen's head slammed into the porch. Sparks flew from the lightning cannon and danced across the timber deck. She banged her fist hard on the steps. A hoof flicked up on to the porch, brushing over her shoulder. Imogen squeezed the trigger on the cannon and punched it into the steps. The front legs buckled then flew up, throwing Imogen into a puddle of pigs' blood on the sloppy ground.

The house came at her with frantic, toothy legs scraping and ripping apart the soil. Imogen switched the cannon to *scorch* and fired at the front of the house. She held her arm up in the general direction of the centipede legs and held her fire until she could no longer feel the feet clawing at the blood-soaked ground.

The house collapsed under an arc of orange flame. Its front legs gave out underneath the porch, falling flat and twitching.

Imogen got to her feet, wiping off the pig-sludge. The house tried to stand. Its front legs pawed the earth like a wounded pup while its functioning legs dug into the ground and dragged it backward. Its front door had been burned clean off its hinges. Scorch marks scored the floor and walls, reaching into the house. Most of the front door lay smoldering in the hall. Its remaining bits still tried to swing on their hinges. The house had finally tasted fear.

The house hunter unclipped her lightning cannon and snapped it to her belt. She walked around the side of the house and ran her palm along the side wall. The house slowly crept backward. A pulse of energy drew Imogen to the laundry window. Her glove hummed and sizzled and snapped, leading her to the house's pressure point—the row of legs buckling to their knees.

A girl appeared in the window above Imogen. The glass shattered outward.

Imogen realized exactly what she was dealing with. She brushed glass out of her hair. The girl had disappeared. Imogen ran to the back of the house. She blasted its back legs with tranquilizers from her glove, slamming the bulk of it to the ground.

Its front legs would soon gain feeling again. Imogen grabbed the hooks and ropes from her pouch. She swung one into a lasso, and slung it over a chimney. The bricks sparked as she cinched it. Imogen staked the other end to the ground. She plucked the rope and it crackled with electricity. She fixed three more ropes to the house with hooks, one through a window on the second floor, where there appeared to be another girl staring out the window. The hook Imogen launched through the window seemed to pass right through the girl. Imogen pulled the rope tight and the hook caught on the wall beside the window.

The house's legs kicked again. It jerked at the ropes. Lightning danced on the roof with each violent tug and burned black marks on the gutters until the house stopped resisting.

Imogen ran to Keith, who leaned on the fence with sweat shining off his forehead. "It's a ghost house," Imogen said.

"What does that mean?" Keith clicked his tongue and a funnel web pony licked his hand through the fence.

"These things are a nightmare, but I can take care of it. It's just… We need to put it down."

"So we're going to have a dead house sitting in the paddock?"

"Yeah. Or I could set you up with some guys I know, removalists."

11

Keith rubbed his brow. "Forget about that for now. What can I do for you now?"

The house struggled. The girl in the laundry room window returned, staring at Imogen and Keith. She had blonde hair and round marks on her face. Her green orb eyes shone like a cat's.

"Get your axe," Imogen said.

Keith brought his axe down on the house's leg. It split and sprayed out a small explosion of splinters. The broken leg twitched on the ground and the house creaked and leaned a little. He swung out in a wide arc and lopped off another leg. The only sounds were Keith's heavy breathing and the constant smack of axe on wood. Imogen stepped up on the porch and stared down the burned hall. She stepped over the door. The hall led right through to the back door. To the left was the laundry where the girl had been watching.

Keith moved to the side of the house, amputating the match-stick legs.

Imogen looked into the laundry room. The girl stood there, staring out the window. She had dirty-blonde hair and wore a filthy, faded *Dead Kennedys* shirt—concert dates from the 80s glowed on its back. The girl turned and smiled at Imogen. Her nose was pierced, and she sported a glimmering red gem. She had big purple bruises on her neck. She waved at Imogen. There was a spider tattoo on the girl's wrist.

Imogen opened her mouth to speak, but there was a grinding noise from outside, and the door slammed shut as the house lurched to the right. Imogen fell against the gray, peeling-papered wall. She tumbled onto the worn, loose floorboards. The house was quiet—damp, suddenly dark, and very quiet.

Imogen pulled out her flashlight and hefted her nail-bat. She stood, balancing against the listed wall, and pushed open the laundry room door with the bat. The room was empty.

"Hello?" she said.

It was the house pulling tricks on her. This was a game. Hide and seek. A maze. Imogen went through the laundry room and into the empty kitchen. A patch of mold on the floor marked the missing refrigerator's place.

Imogen left the kitchen through a hole in the wall that led to a bedroom. Outside the window lay a bundle of broken legs and an axe in the trampled paddock. A single shoe lay at the end of deep furrows in the ground. Imogen turned her attention to the walls of the room. She took a deep breath and tried to connect to the house, to sense its cerebrum.

Somewhere inside, there was something that contained all the house's thoughts, emotions, and memories. The thing that controlled its actions. Imogen sought the source of the poisoned spirit of the house. The cerebrum.

The house hunter tucked her bat under her arm and waved her hand through the air to pick up any electrical disturbances. She tried to feel it in the wall. There was only the crackling of her glove receiving static, the numbing of her hand. Nothing.

Dust floated through flashlight beam, swirling as if the house breathed through its walls. The wallpaper was a series of interconnected suns and moons, gold on navy blue. Knowing smiles shone on all their faces. They looked at Imogen as if to say, "She's not here."

She went into the hall.

Wind rushed through the front door, stirring dust and splinters up the stairs. Imogen felt a light pull on her hand. She clipped her lightning cannon back on to her wrist, and followed the tug of her glove, climbing the stairs behind the gust of wind—bat raised. She noticed that the frames lining the walls of the stairway were devoid of photographs.

The second-floor landing was cold. The air was suffocating. It pulled the warmth from Imogen's face. Most of the doorways sealed and papered to match the hall—black spiders on white. They seemed to follow Imogen as she explored. She reminded herself it was just the house pulling tricks on her.

Imogen came to a door that hadn't been patched over.

13

Her hand hummed and crackled. Sparks shot off the nails at the end of the bat. She opened the door to an orchestra of screams. A blonde girl wearing filthy pink polka-dot pajamas grappled at the window on the far wall. The electric hook that Imogen had thrown through the window sunk into the back of her head and protruding from her right eye-socket. The ghost girl had both feet propped on the wall, straddling the shattered window. She struggled to free her head and keep from falling out the window.

"Help me," she said. "Please, help me!"

"What are you doing here?"

"My sister…my uncle was…FUCKING BASTARD! He was fucking… locked me in here! Now this hook. Please get it out. I need to find her."

The room shook and tiles tumbled off the roof. Imogen raised her bat. The air smelled of ozone.

The girl wailed like a banshee. "Aren't you going to help me?" She cried.

Imogen shook her head. "You're the cerebrum, aren't you?" She slung the bat over her shoulder.

"What are you doing? You've got to help me!" The girl grabbed the rope and tugged. She twisted and ripped at the hook, screaming as it burned and sizzled in her head, lighting up her skull with blue-white fire. A sick jerk pulled the hook loose, and it flung out the window, taking half-her face with it. The house lurched. Imogen and the girl fell.

The closet door sprung open, revealing a mangled mess of flesh and bone. Keith's corpse, bloodied and torn up, lay among pig parts. His face was slack. His red eyes were vacant.

The girl lunged.

Imogen swung her bat at the girl's head. The girl flipped sideways with a dull crack as bat connected, driving nails into her skull. Imogen let go of her weapon and the girl bounced on the floor. Blood bubbled from her lips.

"Please," she said, reaching for Imogen's ankles. "Why won't you help me?"

Imogen fired her lightning cannon into the girl. The girl's skin turned pale white and exploded.

The house crashed to the ground. There was a snapping sound, and the air cleared. Wood creaked and sighed and there was stillness. Imogen picked up her bat and put it in her bag. She dragged what was left of Keith out of the closet and carried him outside. Dumping the body in the muck, she went back to the house and pulled the doorknob from the charred front door. She slipped the lump of brass into her pocket.

Imogen dragged Keith's body to Mary, who came crying from the porch.

2

THE RHINO AND THE ASSASSIN

Mary paid Imogen three bags of chicken feed. Imogen snuck a fourth on her way out. It wasn't a lot, but she could barter with it. Maybe get food. Soap. Her clothes were soaked with mud and pig's blood, and it was drying quickly in the cool morning air. She would need a lot of soap.

Imogen stopped at the Twenty-Four Seven on her way home. The shopkeeper was a cockroach-man. He swivelled his tiny head—a shiny black-domed thing with tiny black eyes spiralled with brown. Two long antennae extended from the top of his head, twitching and groping. He had his hairy feet up on the counter, with two arms behind his head, and two tossing butterfly chips into his segmented mouth.

A rerun of *Married With Children*—from the old times—played on a tiny TV on the counter.

The shopkeeper stared at Imogen. He put down his chips and gawked at her as she approached the counter. "What do you want?"

Imogen stared at the cockroach man. She unslung her pack and dropped it on the floor.

"What do you want?" he repeated.

Imogen rummaged through her bag. She put the feed on the counter. "Some soap and beans."

He picked up a bag, inspecting it.

"And some chocolate, too."

The shopkeeper grunted. "A bar of soap, a tin of beans."

"What? That's ridiculous."

"That's—" The bug man's antennae shot straight up in the air. He stared past Imogen, though the tiny front window. "Oh, shit," he said.

Imogen turned.

16

A mammoth rhino walker ran straight for the store. It slammed into the wall and Imogen was thrown through the front door. She rolled and bounced on the pavement with shards of glass and chunks of brick.

The rhino stomped backward, nearly trampling her. It reared for another run.

But the store was on its feet, lurching forward on eight thick legs as the rhino walker charged. The rhino adjusted its course and chased after the nimble convenience store.

Imogen stumbled for her spider walker and joined the race. Her stuff was still inside that store.

She caught up to them in the warehouse district near the port. These were some of the biggest buildings in the city—block after block of nothing but factory or dispatch warehouse. Tall concrete walls and barbed-wire fences bordered the street.

The convenience store came tearing around a corner and ran straight at her. Imogen tried to make it to the next intersection, to side-step the thing. The rhino walker came bursting from the other side of the street, though, and barrelled into the runaway building, smashing it through a concrete wall. It tumbled and struggled to get up.

The rhino's driver yelled down at Imogen, "Go! Get out of here."

Imogen sat still as the rhino backed up and charged the crippled store again. This time its horn glowed green with the energy of a heavy lightning cannon. Whoever the guy was, he meant to hurt that store. Maybe even kill it.

The rhino walker bashed into the building, discharging its weapon. The convenience store jumped and its legs kicked. It didn't move after that.

The man climbed out of his walker. "Go!" he said, waving his arm wildly at Imogen. He wore a black cap over shoulder-length gray hair. His face was mostly gray whiskers, with faded diamond markings that tracked down his face like scales. He went to the busted-in door saying,

"If you're not gone when I'm done here, I'm coming for you next. Get out of here."

Imogen slid off her walker. "That piece of shit cockroach in there's got my stuff. I need it back."

The man stopped and turned toward her. "Beat it."

"I'm not leaving without my stuff."

He scratched his nose and pointed his lightning cannon at her. "Your stuff or your life."

Imogen stared down his cannon. "I—"

The man flicked his wrist and she heard the whine of his weapon charging.

She climbed on her spider walker and left.

3
THE STRANGER

When Imogen turned into her street, she could sense something dangerous in the atmosphere. The dirt path to her house had been used recently. She took off her goggles, folded up her spider walker, and walked through the front yard.

She knew someone was inside. Her house was like a fortress. A fortress. It had been torn wide open.

Imogen found the front door unlocked and waiting for her. She whispered her house's name, "Sonica". Her house was like a fucking fortress.

She stroked her finger on the door and felt the invisible cracks that ran outward like a spider web. She traced it to the point where the door had been broken. Her hand pressed against the wood where the intruder's hand had done its work.

Imogen pressed her ear to the door and a voice said, "Come inside."

When she obliged, the voice said, "Welcome home, Imogen. I was getting a little worried about you."

A man sat in her chair. There was a body slumped at his feet and Imogen's broken bag rested on his lap. His hair curtained down around his face and his nose looked like it had been broken three or four times, at least. He wore a white shirt with the sleeves rolled up, showing the scars up and down his arms, and black leather gloves. The body at his feet was bleeding too much to still be alive. It was a tall, young woman with short red hair and a red face with a thin blue stripe and big golden eyes. Her nostrils were slits, and her eyebrows were shiny, short black horns.

"I parked my rhino beetle in the swamp out the back. I

19

hope you don't mind," the man said. He was eating beans from a tin and he took a mouthful and winked at Imogen.

"Who are you?" Imogen asked.

"Here," the man lifted the bag from his lap. "This belongs to you, I believe." He tossed it over to Imogen.

"Thanks." She opened the bag and flicked through the contents. She tied the straps back together and pulled them tight.

"Yes," he said. "Name's Ellis. And I'm glad I got to you before *they* did." He scowled and kicked the woman on the floor.

"And who are *they*?"

"Agents from the House Hunter Association. Lucky this one was just an amateur."

Imogen stared at the woman on the carpet and nodded.

"Tell me," Ellis said. "How long did you think they'd let you continue as a free agent?"

Stare. That puddle of blood was going to stain.

"You've been cleaning up their mess and cutting into their profits." Ellis kicked the woman again.

"I'm just doing my job! I got my permits, my house hunting license. They've got no right." Imogen cradled her head in her hands.

"No, they don't. But that won't stop them. And don't think you're the only one. They're after all of us."

"What do they want?"

"They're trying to bring back the Davinson Initiative."

"What makes them think it'll work this time around?"

"The rumors are that this time they'll have the Jabberhouse."

"Bullshit." Imogen sat on the floor and leaned against the wall.

"As far as I can tell, it's true. I've been tracking them for months." Ellis took off his glasses and rubbed his eyes. "And I've visited so many homes just like yours. The homes of skilled house hunters. But every time I've been too late." Ellis finished his beans and took the tin into the kitchen. "You know, that ghost house you took care of down at Funnel Web Farm. That house belonged to one of the house hunters I was watching. But the agents got to her first. Tortured the poor girl to lure more of you out. It was a trap, Imogen. They paid off the Nolans." He returned to his seat.

"So," Imogen said. "What happens now that you've *got* one of us? What do you want from me?"

"I need your help. I need to find the Jabberhouse before they do."

"Ridiculous. Where's the proof it actually exists?"

"What if I had proof? What if I told you I'm secretly building an army to bring down the Association?"

Imogen sighed and tilted her head against the wall. "Are you?"

"No. Not really. I've been keeping a low profile. I didn't want the Association coming after me, too. I've just been trying to get to the free agents without the Association knowing."

"So why did you step in now? Why'd you bring a dead agent into my house? Who the hell *are* you?"

"It was either I kill her or she killed you. She failed with the ghost house. I followed her following you. She was inside that store, and about to nab you. She's an amateur, but she still lured you to their safe house in the warehouse district. You're lucky I stopped her when I did."

"What happens once they notice she's gone missing?"

Ellis shrugged. "They send more agents after you, I suppose. I'm sure she sent a report before I got to her. They've got your number."

"So what happens now?"

"I think we can help each other out here. I can protect you from the Association. Just help me find the Jabberhouse."

"It's a legend."

"Legends have got to come from somewhere, Imogen. It's just been hiding from us for too long."

"And what of all the other house hunters you've been tracking? You want to leave them to defend themselves while you and I wander off on a hunch that some mythical creature exists, and that we're the ones to find it?"

"Most of them are dead already. You're the first one I've found that's actually fought them off. I don't expect you to

S. T. Cartledge

buy into all this right away. But I think you should come
with me. You've done all right so far on your own, but it
won't last."

"Do you have anything to go on? Anything at all?"

Ellis smiled. "Of course."

"What happened to the shopkeeper?"

"Who?"

"The cockroach-man."

"He was a slick mess on the floor."

Imogen nodded. "Good."

4
HOUSEJACKED

Imogen didn't wake until early morning the next day. Her house was moving. She stumbled to the window and found that they were on the highway

"Ellis! What's going on? Where are you?"

"Out here," he said.

"What the fuck are you doing with Sonica?" Imogen snatched the bear off the table.

"We're going to Huntsman City. We talked about this yesterday."

"Sonica?"

"My house. My fucking house, you shit. What do you think you're doing?"

"I dumped the agent in the swamp. You were fast asleep. We needed to get moving, so I found your spider-bear and now she's taking us to the city. We thought we would let you get a full night's rest."

"It's *my* house! You can't just decide you want to go for a late night joyride. You just can't do shit like that." Imogen clutched her spider-bear tight. "I control Sonica, not you. You want to do anything, go anywhere, you talk to me, I talk to her."

"We don't have time to waste. The Association– "

"You talk to me, I talk to her. Yeah?"

Ellis nodded. "She stung me pretty good the first time."

"That's why I've got precautions in the first place. I don't trust you."

"Yeah."

Imogen sat down on the other side of the table. "If you're going to be eating my food, you'd better go cook some up for me too."

"I've just been eating them cold."

"Go."

"There's no getting out of searching for the Jabberhouse. You understand that part, right?"

Imogen stroked the spider-bear's fur and sighed. "Yes. What's in Huntsman City that's going to help us track down this Jabberhouse?"

"I know a guy who knows things."

"Who?"

"A monk. Of the Order of the Architects"

"Huh?"

"You know. Bald man, wears a robe, lives in a temple. His temple is right in the city. We should get in by mid-afternoon."

By noon they hit the outer suburbs. There were small, run-down houses on unstable legs wandering around their neighborhoods; tripping and stumbling, windows smashed in, walls dented. One house had a collapsed roof.

"What is this?" Imogen said.

"You thought White Tail was bad?" Ellis said.

Imogen hugged her spider-bear as a little blue cottage ran away from them.

"This is pretty much normal," Ellis said.

"This is horrible," Imogen said.

A house-fighting ring lay ahead. Two houses fought in the center—smashing and splintering each other while people crowded around cheering and yelling. Men and women in filthy business suits waved fists full of money and shouted at each other. Imogen couldn't tell who was more savage—the houses or the humans. Some of the people watched Sonica walk past. Imogen thought they looked crazy.

"Ignore them," Ellis said.

Farther along there were houses tipped over in the middle of the street like they were maybe abused or they had just fallen over and didn't know how to get back up. And no one seemed to notice.

"See what's happening here, Imogen?" Ellis said. "Look at that and tell me it doesn't tear you up inside."

Two small suburban houses were fighting. One had its front pair of legs wrapped around the support beams of the other house. It ripped them out and took out half its roof with it. Inside, people screamed for the houses to stop.

Imogen had seen plenty of houses that had problems wandering in the night, or brawling houses in the wild, but this was on a completely different scale.

There were *people* inside. And they didn't have any idea what to do.

"Ellis, we need to help them," Imogen said, leaning over the railing as Sonica walked past.

"We can't get involved."

"Those people need us."

"Listen, Imogen. I know this sounds harsh, but everyone needs help. We'd get nowhere if we stopped for everyone that needed us. Keep walking."

"You know, this is all because of that Davinson prick. A whole generation of houses bred in captivity. This is the sort of shit that happens."

"For what it's worth, I'm sorry. We've just got to pick our battles."

Deeper into the city, the fighting and destruction was worse. The inner city was a warzone of chaos and shrapnel. Not a single road was free of rubble, not a block of land free of scars A three-story hospital had been reduced to half-a-story. An apartment building wandered around on clumsy Bambi legs, staggering into smaller buildings before toppling over in a disoriented haze.

A shopping center had transformed into a concrete jungle. Chains of shops linked together and stacked up and running full sprint at other chains of shops like juggernauts, crumbling to debris on impact and embracing the wild nature of their monstrous existence in not-giving-a-fuck. Whole sections of the shopping center fell as Imogen, Ellis and Sonica walked past.

Even if the Jabberhouse turned out to be fake, Imogen felt it was her place to try and mend the city, to right the relationships between man and house. As it was, walking past the smouldering embers of a district primary school, there was no pride or affection. The people showed no responsibilities to their home and work, to their schools, or institutions.

Ellis gave directions while Imogen navigated Sonica through the streets safely; sidestepping fallen buildings, backing her way around intense brawls, and just outright fleeing the buildings that were hell-bent on destruction. Finally, they stood before the temple.

5

THE TEMPLE OF THE ARCHITECTS

It stood tall in the center of the city, with great curling spires decorated in gold and crimson patterns. Massive stained glass windows stretched along the front of the building, depicting elaborate buildings in fantastic foreign lands. One showed a short, wide, cylindrical house walking across a lake of fire. And had a giant pyramid leading a pack of other pyramids through a valley toward the ocean.

The doors to the temple must have been about five stories high. They were dark and heavy. Brass bars running ran along their width. Imogen stepped off her porch and stared. She threw her weight against the doors and they didn't budge.

"You'll be needing Sonica to help you with that," Ellis said.

She hadn't thought of it, but the entrance was wide enough to fit a house through.

"I'd like to see just how strong this little house is," Ellis said, knocking on the wood.

Imogen returned to the porch and picked up her spider-bear. Her fingers gently gripped the pink toy. It trembled a little. Sonica stepped up to the doors and pushed her front legs against the beams. Timber creaked and Imogen squeezed the spider-bear tighter. The windows shivered, the roof tiles rattled, Sonica lunged forward with a loud structural groan, then slumped against the unmoved temple doors.

"You're better than this," Ellis said. "You can do it."

"Yeah, I know."

"Concentrate. Don't force it. Don't push it. Make Sonica want to do the pushing."

"I know what I'm doing." Imogen wiped sweat off her forehead and ran her fingers through the spider-bear's fur,

27

over its face.

The house pushed against the doors, her back feet digging into the ground.

"Come on," Imogen said. "Come on!" She smacked her palm against the house.

Ellis said, "Try it without your gloves. See how your spider-bear responds to your skin."

"But the gloves amplify the connection."

"I know how they work. Just try it."

Imogen rolled her eyes and tucked her hair behind her ear. She took off her gloves and stuffed them in her breast pocket, shaking her head. Her fingers curled around the spider-bear just beneath its second set of arms. Its pink synthetic fur was soft. Its body was warm, with electric energy rubbing off on her skin.

"This is your house," Ellis said. "Own it."

Sonica shivered. She crept back from the doors.

Imogen wrapped her arms around the spider-bear and stared at the temple's sealed entry. Sonica took a feeble step forward. Sonica lurched forward, almost crashing into the doors. Imogen wiped a sweaty palm on her shorts and puller her house back upright.

Imogen panted. Her face flushed pink, and its pale hexagon lines grew darker. Her little plush toy pulsed and sparked blue. Imogen's hands were hot and slippery on the spider-brear. Sonica charged against the temple doors. Again, creaking timber, rattling windows and roof tiles. Sonica's front door swung open and slammed shut. Her steel legs slipped on the ground, digging in.

"Come on," Imogen muttered. "Come on, come on . . ."

"Imogen," Ellis said. "Relax. You're doing it again."

Imogen looked down at the spider-bear. She clawed the toy.

"Don't force it. Let Sonica do the pushing."

Imogen slowly unclenched her fingers. She stopped trying to force things and just stared at the glowing spider-bear. Its charged fur reached into her fingertips. The house linked with her completely. The blue sparks from the plush toy cerebrum climbed up Imogen's arms, and the hexagon markings on her face flashed with its light. Imogen's vision turned white, like she was dumped in a milky sea. She could feel the cold brass of the temple doors through Sonica's feet, and the cracked asphalt beneath her back legs, gripping. Sonica backed away again and charged at the temple doors. Her front legs braced against the beams while her back legs held steady and pushed. The giant temple doors swung slowly open.

Beyond the door lay a long hallway draped with purple curtains. A red carpet on its floor led into darkness.

The spider-bear stopped glowing blue, but maintained a dull electrical hum, a luminescence. Sonica walked down the hall. Then she ambled down the hall gathering speed until she was running in a full sprint. The temple seemed impossibly vast.

The hall curved to the right. Then there was a sharp turn right, and then another right. They followed a series of right corners folding in on themselves without spiralling in or out or crossing over. Perhaps this was a trick of the building's design, to give the appearance of going somewhere. More right turns. Then: Stairs.

These were massive house stairs, about three feet high per step, and about a hundred and fifty feet wide. Sonica launched herself up the stairs, one giant step at a time. The staircase ended at a long, wide room that was filled with people and houses, all looking pretty run-down.

The floor was a polished green marble and there were thick white pillars with detailed carvings of great winged buildings soaring around a giant city in the clouds, and a fire-breathing estate house repelling a tribe of pygmy-houses, cast to life by the light and the shadows in the etchings. Tall buildings like dragons curling around every second pillar. The red carpet continued down the middle of the hall. Sonica trotted along it.

Eyes watched them from huge nooks, crevices and

doorways lining the hall—faces shadowed by hoods. Monks in dark robes sat in front of houses built into them, facing the center of the hall. Imogen noticed an occasional dark green or blue or red robed person with their hood thrown back. The people wearing those robes had pale faces, eye-shaped markings all over their skin, and white hair crafted into mohawks, devil horns, decorative buns, ponytails, fountainheads, bird's nests and explosive Einsteins. All wild, all white, all staring at Imogen and Ellis and Sonica.

Sonica reached the end of the hall and a monk jumped onto the porch. She sat beside Imogen and Ellis.

"Brother Joshua has been waiting for you," the monk said. She was a tall, young woman with orange compound eyes and Warhol hair.

"Thank you," Ellis said with a small nod.

"Who are these people?" Imogen whispered. She was looking into a vast, dimly-lit room, where people and houses mingled.

"Most of them are homeless," he said. "Their houses have been destroyed."

Even the houses looked homeless.

Brother Joshua sat near the center of the room on a tall, intricately carved bird house. He wore a green robe that spilled over the bird house. His long white hair spilled over his shoulders. His face looked like a young boy's— no eyebrows, no wrinkles. His eyes were like giant white moons reflected in smoky water, shining toward Sonica.

The bird house stood on thousands of long, thin spaghetti legs that clumped together into writhing stalks, slipping off its perch to meet the guests. A door on the front of the bird house swung open and a wooden hand slid out. A silver canary sat on its finger.

The canary flew to Sonica's porch railing. Ellis held out his hand, and the bird chirped brightly and hopped onto his finger. He brought it over to Imogen, who ran a finger over its tiny head.

"Do you feel that?" he said.

A little white spark jumped from the bird's beak to Imogen's finger.

"It's his cerebrum, yeah?" she said.

"Yes," the monk on the porch said. "Brother Joshua possesses great power and discipline."

"Beautiful, isn't it?" Ellis said. The canary flew from his finger and darted around the room.

"Welcome, my brother and sister, to the temple of the Architects," Joshua said, the bird house leaning close to Sonica. "What is it that you seek?"

"Brother Joshua, We're looking for the Jabberhouse." Ellis said.

"Ah, my friend. The Jabberhouse is dead."

"I hear the House Hunter Association is searching for it."

"Control the houses, and you control the cities. They want to give birth to new cities of their own grand designs."

"But what can they do if the Jabberhouse is dead?"

"They're an organization with many secrets. They can do many things. The death of the Jabberhouse is not the end. Even dead, that great house holds power. They will still search for it, and use what they can of it for their goals."

"I'll find a way to stop them. I have to. The world they want to create… We can't go through that again. It doesn't work. It's barbarous. We know what their future holds."

"The Davinson Initiative taught us about the nature of houses, yes. But do *you* know better than Charles Davinson?" Joshua gazed towards Ellis, his pearly eyes unflinching.

Ellis spat on the ground. "I don't give a shit about that man's knowledge. His research should be vanquished from history."

Joshua said, "Perhaps his recent death will help to start that process." The old man's pearly eyes widened. "Were you aware that he had died?"

Ellis wiped his mouth on his sleeve and met Joshua's gaze. "What else can you tell us about the Jabberhouse?"

"I have my information. But first, I need to know you're ready for it."

The silver canary flew back to the wooden hand and withdrew into the bird house.

"I'm sure you saw the buildings brawling in the city?" Joshua said.

31

Ellis nodded.

"Barbaric. It takes a great deal more skill and determination to engage an Architect in a fair fight." Joshua's house-hand came back out of the bird house, pointing at the porch. "You will fight Sadie. House versus house. Architect rules. Sadie is an expert in structural origami. If you beat her, I'll tell you what I know."

"Me?" Ellis said.

"No," Joshua replied. "Her." He nodded at Imogen.

6
BATTLE

The arena was a large rectangle with red marble floors and gold running around the edges. There were two massive doorways at either end and it was surrounded by high walls. Joshua sat on his bird house on a little golden branch up high on the wall. Above him, all around there were people and houses sitting and watching the floor as Imogen brought Sonica into the arena through one door while Sadie brought her house in through the other.

Sadie's house was no taller than Sonica but it was thin, and it walked on three long legs with backwards knees like bird legs. Its wall panels folded and fluttered like feathers, moving with a grace that was quite crane-like. Beautiful and majestic, it looked like it might be able to fly. Imogen had heard of rare breeds of flying houses living in far off, exotic parts of the world, but had never seen one before.

Sadie brushed her fingers through her hair and walked up to Imogen. Her house sat down, waiting back. "We won't be in our houses when we fight them." Sadie laughed. Her eyes were like honeycombs. "Don't look so worried. The way we do things here, it's a harmless spectator sport. More or less."

"More or less?"

"I'm not making any promises."

Imogen turned away from Sadie's unblinking eyes and unbroken smile. *Hate to ruin that pretty face*, she thought. She searched the crowd for Ellis but couldn't find him. Cuddling her spider-bear, Imogen sat down on her front steps.

Sonica was a nice house, but she just looked kind of washed out in contrast to Sadie's house. Off-white. Old. Battered. Tired. Wrinkled skin starting to sag, ageing in front

33

of everyone. In front of the young one. Imogen and Sadie would have been close to the same age, but their houses were a generation apart. Imogen closed her eyes and Ellis' face crawled into her head.

"Your cerebrum has never left your house, has it?" Sadie asked.

Imogen shrugged. "Not really."

"It's no big deal. It's a little awkward at the start, but you get used to it pretty quick."

Imogen nodded. "What's that?" She pointed at the jar nestled in Sadie's arms. "Is that yours?" The jar was full of a greenish liquid, with what looked like a baby pig floating in it, pale gray, curled up, eyelids like slits ballooned out. And the little extra head poking out the side and two more little hoofs poking out the other side.

Sadie nodded. "It's a pickled punk. Got it at a carnival. When I found Charlotte, it just seemed like the right thing for her cerebrum."

"I've had my spider-bear since I was a baby," Imogen said, lifting it up. "He was my binky. He's been patched up a few times, and he's been through the wash more times than I can remember, but I wouldn't go with anything else for Sonica."

"Yeah, you'll be fine," Sadie said. She shook Imogen's hand.

Sadie went over to one side of the arena and climbed a ladder to a high chair that overlooked it. She sat there with her pickled punk and waited for Imogen to climb up to her chair.

Imogen shivered in the chair and hugged her binky.

"Are you ready?" Joshua asked, looking across to Sadie and then to Imogen. Imogen gulped and nodded. "Begin!" Joshua's voice filled the arena and a roar of applause flared up.

Imogen held her spider-bear tight, its fur electrified, and Sonica took her first few steps without Imogen inside. Charlotte sat still, waiting for Sonica to approach. Imogen's heart beat like mad and she took deep breaths, trying to keep her focus, to keep Sonica walking steady. Sadie had her fingers delicately wrapped around her jar of mutant pig fetus, a twitch of a smile on her face.

Sonica paused, took a couple more steps, standing tall, then charged at Charlotte. With speed and grace, Charlotte sidestepped out of the way and Sonica skidded on the floor to keep from tipping over. Charlotte stretched her legs and walked down the length of the arena. She turned around to face Sonica. Her ground floor trembled a little and a wooden fist sprung out of the window and launched itself at Sonica, striking her on the side, punching a hole into her kitchen. Imogen cried out. Her whole body shook. Electric spasms pulled her muscles tight. She took in big wheezing breaths, eyes watering.

Charlotte trembled again and pulled another wooden fist out of the window, letting it hang there for a moment like a threat. She fired again, this time striking closer to Sonica's back, punching a hole into her bedroom.

Imogen's head was tilted over her spider-bear, her shoulders bobbing up and down. Tears dribbled down her face, dripped onto her cerebrum and sizzled to steam. Imogen let out a cry that echoed through the arena.

Charlotte sat back down and waited for Imogen to collect herself, and for Sonica to get back on her feet. A third fist was cocked and ready to fire.

Imogen wiped her eyes on her sleeve, deep blue and shining, and slowly Sonica got back on her legs. The fist fired and Sonica leapt away. The fist went crashing into the arena wall. Imogen's fingers gripped her spider-bear tight, and she sniffed and thought about what Ellis said out the front of the temple. Her hands were shaking. She unclenched her fingers and thought about Sonica growing arms to punch that Charlotte in her stupid window.

More fists, and Sonica was running and dodging them. They cracked into the wall, leaving spider-web patterns. Boards from Sonica's insides patched up her holes. Walls shifted for the renovations. Shrinking a little bit, she charged at Charlotte again. Her porch came loose and swept at her opponent's side, but Charlotte leapt over Sonica and dropped a limestone egg from her foundations through Sonica's roof. Charlotte fluttered over her and landed in the middle of the arena.

Sonica trembled. Her roof tiles snaked back over themselves, broken tiles popping out and sliding to the floor, and Sonica trembled. Charlotte sat facing Sonica and folded herself down a bit. Sonica trembled.

The limestone egg shot from Sonica's back door and smashed through Charlotte's front. Sadie grunted. Two big fists burst from Sonica's sides. They were big and black with brass knuckles. They swung on a series of springs and hinges.

Charlotte began to transform again, too. She folded down flat and sprung back up as an origami tiger-house, white walls with black stripes. Her roof arched up as she stretched her big, powerful legs. The front room opened up like a mouth, thousands of jagged bits of hardwood teeth snapping at Sonica. Charlotte crouched low to the ground and her white walls flushed a deep orange, and she leaped at Sonica.

Sonica grabbed Charlotte by the jaws, her fists wrapped around thick, gummy beams, the hardwood cutting into her fingers, red, sap-like saliva trickling over knuckles. She wrenched the jaws apart and swung Charlotte aside. Charlotte slid across the floor, turned and sprinted back.

This time, Sonica ducked out of the way and swung a backhand at Charlotte. It brushed her side, and Sonica slipped over. Charlotte gripped her leg and twisted it

Imogen cried out as Charlotte turned it further around. It felt like Imogen's own leg was twisting and splintering in the claws. Sonica swung her fist repeatedly at Charlotte. She connected with Charlotte's head and punched repeatedly until she let go. She ripped the front of Charlotte's roof off, and Sadie screamed. Charlotte collapsed on her side.

Sonica limped down the arena away from Charlotte. She turned and Charlotte was standing again, firing a string of tiny cast-iron fists at Sonica. They pummelled into her and she collapsed. Charlotte's back arched, teeth bared, roof tiles fluttered forward, covering the hole in her head.

Sadie called across the room, "Just say when and we'll call the match."

36

"No," Imogen replied. The light in her spider-bear pulsed and sizzled, and Sonica stood back up.

Charlotte charged, and Sonica put her arms up to block. Teeth dug into her arm and thrashed and tugged and tore and pulled it off. Charlotte lunged forward and clamped on to the other arm and ripped it off too. Imogen screamed and cried and her face flushed red and her arms went numb and flooded with pins and needles. Charlotte backed away then charged at Sonica's unguarded porch, driving her into a corner and ramming her against the wall and swiping at her support beams with steel claws.

"Are we done?" Sadie asked.

Imogen sobbed quietly.

"Are we done?" Sadie asked.

Charlotte folded down and came up an origami gorilla-house. She picked Sonica up by her leg, ceiling scraping against the arena floor.

"Yes!" Imogen screamed. "We're done," she said. "We're done."

Joshua proclaimed Sadie the winner and the crowd cheered.

Charlotte put Sonica down and set her upright. Imogen's house came over to her and slumped over and Imogen tried to climb down from her chair but her body was shaking too much. She sat there for a moment and clumsily went about repairing her house.

7
BROTHER JOSHUA

"Hey, no hard feelings, right?" Sadie said.

"Yeah."

"You did a pretty good job for a newcomer." Sadie left the arena and waved for Imogen to follow.

"Thanks."

They were in a large room with a couple of benches in the middle and black bowls filled with hot water sitting on the floor.

"You got a pretty good house," Sadie said.

"Thanks."

"I mean it. And, uh, good luck searching for the Jabberhouse."

They sat down with their cerebra beside them. Sadie dunked a wash cloth in one of the bowls, and wiped her face. She passed a wash cloth to Imogen.

"Thanks, but I can't see us finding it now." Imogen dunked her wash cloth and slapped it over her head. Warm water trickling through her hair and down her neck.

"What, because you lost a fight?" Sadie wrung her cloth out and rubbed her face with it.

"We don't have any information to work with."

"You'll find something."

Imogen sighed and wiped the dripping wash cloth down her face. "Why did he have to come to *me*?"

"Who?"

She dropped the wash cloth in her bowl. "Ellis."

"Oh, that old geezer. What's wrong with him?"

"Everything was fine, right? I had my job, I had my life how I liked it. Then he comes along, and now I'm off on a random chase for some bogus faery-house, and it's like he's

38

expecting me to fight all his battles for him."

"Where you from?"

"White Tail."

"Probably wouldn't have lasted much longer. The good life. You know, what with the Association coming through and stirring shit up. And the Structural Anxiety Disorder that's spreading like the plague, it hasn't reached White Tail yet?"

"It did. Kind of. Fuck, why couldn't things just go back to normal?" Imogen stood up and kicked her bowl across the room. "I've got nowhere to go."

"What is normal?" Sadie said.

Imogen sat down again.

Sadie leaned forward and put her hand on Imogen's back. "Here's not the worst of it, honey. You'll be fine, especially with a skillset like yours."

Ellis stood in the doorway at the end of the room and said, "Brother Joshua wants to see us. When you're ready."

"It'll be okay," Sadie said.

"Thanks." Imogen picked up her spider-bear and followed Ellis out.

"I'm sorry," she said.

"It's okay," Ellis replied.

"I just don't —"

"It's okay. Really."

Brother Joshua waited for them outside a long hallway, wearing a black robe. The silver canary sat on his shoulder.

"Imogen, wonderful effort," he said. "Please, I would like you both to come with me." He motioned down the hallway. "To my meditation chamber."

The hall was filled with streets of glass houses, hundreds of them, with a few dozen monks wandering among them. Each house had a unique shape and design, and they all seemed to reflect each other and pass through each other and bounce wild angles off each other like an explosion in a crystal cave.

"Beautiful, aren't they?" Joshua said. "This is our glass house sanctuary. We raise them from infancy right through full maturity here. They're just not meant to survive in the wild, too fragile, so we do all that we can to nurture them ourselves."

"Where did Sadie learn to fight like that?" Imogen asked.

"It's not what they teach you at the House Hunter's Academy, is it?" Joshua said.

Imogen shook her head.

"We've got our own methods of house training. We've got a few tricks most people don't know about. You adapted quite well to Sadie's fighting style. With a bit of training, we could make an architect out of you yet."

"Thank you."

"Houses are wonderful creatures," Joshua said. "Sometimes I wish the Association would do good to remember that. They are precious, delicate creatures. You can't keep them locked up. You must encourage them to live and grow. You must befriend them. When you take its cerebrum and bind it to a token object, you must also bind a part of yourself to it. Only then you will be truly connected to your house. I see that you understand that better than most."

Imogen nodded. "Thank you."

"And remember, Imogen, torture is *never* the right option. It's the secret to the architect's way."

"Yeah," Imogen said. "I don't think that's much of a secret."

Joshua laughed. "Exactly right, my dear, exactly right! The secret is in what these houses are capable of. If the Association knew what we know, there's no doubt they'd exploit it. They're playing a politics game, Imogen, and we're playing with ethics."

Ellis cleared his throat. "Say they find the Jabberhouse. What then?"

"They find it, they get it under control, that's game over," Joshua said.

"So what happens now? What happens with us?" Ellis said.

"You find that Jabberhouse. You find it, and you stop the Association."

40

"Your monks could do so much more than me," Imogen said. "Can't they help us?"

"You give yourself too little credit. Besides, we are needed here. Someone must protect the city." Joshua waved Ellis and Imogen through to his meditation chamber, a small, round room with black, square mats laid out around it. "I think you have earned the right to know what I have heard about the Jabberhouse."

The three sat down and brother Joshua turned to Ellis. "Have you told Imogen about your time in jail yet?"

"What's that got to do with anything?" Ellis said.

"Have you told her?"

"No."

"What happened?" Imogen asked.

"It's nothing. It's not important."

"You need to trust her," Joshua said.

"You didn't, you know, *kill* anyone, did you?" Imogen asked. She tried to make the word sound smaller than it really was.

"No! Nothing like that." Ellis sighed and took his cap off. "I tried to sabotage the Davinson project. Back when I worked for the Association."

"Oh," she said. "I understand."

"Tell her how long the sentence was," Joshua said.

Ellis ran his fingers through his hair. "Why does she need to know all this, Joshua?"

"You need to trust her, Ellis. Otherwise, it will catch up with you eventually."

Ellis glared at Joshua. "I had a life sentence."

"When did they release you?" Imogen asked.

"Last year."

"That must have been at least . . . thirteen, fourteen years?"

"Fifteen."

"You're skimming over the details, Ellis," Joshua said, his white eyes blankly staring Ellis down.

"What more do you know about the Jabberhouse?"

Joshua laughed. "That's it for now? Okay, have it your way. But remember that you'll need to fill in the details some time. Now, the word on the street is that if you make your way down to Cape Firefly, you'll find the town swarming with agents from the Association." He stroked his silver canary and whistled. "I did a bit of digging around and a little bird told me that the Jabberhouse is in the Black Widow Rainforest."

"But you said before, the Jabberhouse is dead, right?" Imogen said. "So where does that leave us?"

"I have also heard that the Davinson project has been developing a lightning cannon with revivifying properties."

Ellis looked stunned. Imogen looked a little confused.

"It means that if they can find the Jabberhouse's cerebrum, they can bring it back to life. And with it they will be able to create cities or tear them to the ground at their leisure. Even your house and our houses will be left to their devices."

"How can we find the Jabberhouse and its cerebrum?" Imogen said. "The Black Widow Rainforest is huge."

"I don't know its exact location," Joshua said, "But I believe it's somewhere not far from the Taipan River. Maybe getting close to Cottonmouth Valley."

"And what does the cerebrum look like?" Ellis asked.

"I don't know. But you should be able to sense its energy. That's all I can tell you."

"Thank you," Ellis said.

Imogen bowed her head. "Thanks."

8
CHESS

"I never mentioned this before," Ellis said, "But brother Joshua was the first person I went to when I got out of jail."

Ellis and Imogen were sitting in Sonica's lounge room as she sat on the southbound train heading for Cape Firefly. The train hauled a string of passenger cars carrying about half a dozen houses.

"What was it like?" Imogen asked.

"Hmm?"

"Jail," Imogen said. "What was it like?"

"Whole lot of nothing, really. Just walls and bars."

Imogen nodded and stared out the window.

"It was the most depressing building I've ever been in," Ellis said. "It really drains everything from you. It was like, the building was unhappy. Like it had been tortured something terrible. And it passed the suffering on to us." Ellis sipped on a hot coffee. "So many people tried killing themselves. So many people. I think that maybe, every way you can try to kill yourself, I've seen it. A new guy moves in and he's just another chump getting consumed by the institution. And I spent all day, every day, trying to convince my cell that it could be happy. That we would be better off if we could focus all our time on creating a special positive energy to share between us."

"How'd you get out of your life sentence?"

"Did a runner on them."

Imogen laughed. "Really?"

"Yeah."

"Is that why you've been keeping a low profile? Because of the search warrants?"

"When you've been there for fifteen years, nothing better

43

to do, you've got plenty of time to plot out your flawless escape plan. So that's what I did. And no one noticed I was gone." Ellis brushed his hair out of his face. "Hey Imogen?"

"Yeah?"

"What made you want to become a house hunter?"

Imogen shrugged. "When I was in school, my best friend Francesca's parents were house hunters. I remember the first time going over to her house. It was so warm and inviting. And the house was full of strange and fascinating things. Artifacts they picked up on their travels." Imogen sighed. "Whenever I went over there, her parents told us stories of their adventures. Chess had heard them all a thousand times, and I'd heard them just about that many. But they never got old. Her family settled down in White Tail for long enough for us to be best friends. And then she was gone. They moved again. And I was caught up in the dream of this wonderful, fantastic life outside of town. A life of adventure. I liked the idea of making a difference in the world. Since then I've never wanted to do anything else."

"And what happened to Chess?"

"She became a house hunter too. Runs in the family. She's based in Redback."

"You still stay in touch with her?"

"I haven't spoken to her in a very long time."

"Would she be keeping up on what's going on around these parts?"

"Probably. I can try to call her if you want."

Ellis shrugged. "It's up to you. Just hope that the Association hasn't got to her."

"Don't say that," Imogen said.

She went out onto the porch and called Chess. Imogen wondered if the Association had been tracking house hunters through Redback. And the longer the phone rang, the more Imogen worried. What if Ellis was right? Each ring came with a tightening of her chest. She had an urgent longing to hear that familiar voice.

The train took Sonica past a few small villages, a couple of ghost towns, and the south-west wildlife reserve, where houses ran free through the however many thousands of acres of bush, playing and growing and mating—eventually returning to the wild where they become fair game for the house hunters. These were the most carefree houses that Imogen had seen in a long time, no stress, tension, or constant threat of punishment.

As the landscape rushed past, Imogen rested against the windowsill—the wind tossing her hair back—and closed her eyes. She slept right through to Cape Firefly.

Like Joshua said, the agents had arrived. They were the ones with the big cameras hanging around their necks and backpacks smothered in tourist paraphernalia and the tell-tale signs of chameleon communication devices curled in their ears. This accounted for most of the people in the station, caught in the crossfire of information coming in and going out. There were eight platforms, with agents reporting back to more cities than Imogen cared to dwell on. It was almost embarrassing how transparent these agents were. It was as though they had nothing to hide.

"Do you think they'll be looking out for us?" Imogen asked.

"Maybe the guys back north," Ellis said. "Unless we were followed, I think we're okay. They'll be looking out for people like us, sure, but I don't think we were followed this far. These guys have got bigger prey to hunt. But it couldn't hurt to keep a low profile. Where are we going?"

"She wants us to meet her at a place called Madam Butterfly's."

"Okay," Ellis said. "I don't think we should hang around too long though. I don't like all these agents hovering around."

They left the station, passing a holiday camp site that was packed with dozens of surveillance houses with aerials and satellites mounted in rows along the roofs. A variety of hi-tech off-road walkers—dragonflies, longhorns, rhinos, stags, and grasshoppers—lined up along the fence, watching Sonica pass through town.

"This place," Ellis said. "Madam Butterfly's. Isn't that a flesh house?"

"Uh, yeah, it is. She wants to meet us in the bar. Apparently there's plenty of gossip passing through there. "

Imogen and Ellis dropped Sonica off at a small campsite, then went to Madame Butterfly's, on the main strip with the pubs, clubs, and restaurants. It was tall and brightly colored. It had the he loose shape and markings of an exotic butterfly. They entered, and the first thing they saw was a woman with long green feelers sticking out of the top of her head. The roots of her feelers disappeared beneath a mass of long, purple hair. Her face was pale and pointed like a china doll, and she smiled with her lips pursed, her cheeks doing all the work. She came down a set of stairs and disappeared into a side room.

The wallpaper was a beige-pink with textured nipples running along it, forming a collage of swirling patterns. The paintings on the wall—hung from pierced nipples—were all of naked insectoid women. One of them had a set of butterfly wings, another was a black woman, black as night, with white cobweb patterns spreading out from her navel. There was another painting of a woman with six eyes on her face marked out in a V-shape, and her back was encased in a long, rainbow shell.

This was a place of sweat, lust, and fetish. An insect fetish. Imogen would be happy so long as she could just get through life without coming across a cockroach-man ever again. She led Ellis over to the bar.

There were a few men sitting around the bar and a couple of groups at tables, but there was barely any noise going on. Quiet background music. Some variety of ambient jazz. Private conversations and small mutterings kept hush-hush. Chameleons in their ears.

The bartender was a tall, bald man with light brown skin and big black compound eyes. A woman sat at the bar, curly black hair concealing her face and flowing down to her waist, drinking a Roach Cider.

"Chess?" Imogen said.

The black-haired woman looked up from her drink. She

pulled her hair back around her pointed ears, revealing a pale face with maroon-red eyes and thin nostril slits. Her skin shimmered like a polished seashell and her eyes locked on to Imogen, her dark lips parting into a deep grin.

"Imogen! Come over here. Let me get you a drink." She held up two fingers to the bartender and said, "Pablo. Two Black Widow Ales for my friends here."

"How are you, Chess?" Imogen asked.

Francesca said, "It's been so long, and that's all you have to say?" Francesca passed the frothy blue drinks to Imogen and Ellis. "Don't worry about it. I'm fine, Imogen. You got bigger things going on than to play catch up with old friends. Shall we grab a table?"

One mouthful convinced Imogen the drink wasn't for her. It was sour and bitter and burned its way down the throat. She coughed and covered her mouth, then drank with little cautious sips. The brew didn't seem to have an effect on Ellis, one way or another.

"So," Francesca said. "You sounded urgent on the phone. What brings you out here?"

"Yeah, about that, Chess, if anyone comes asking about us, we don't really know you. We're down here on a holiday. We're looking for a sea change. Or something. Yeah?"

Francesca nods. "Yeah, so what's the job?"

"It's a little tricky," Imogen said. "Let's just say there's a corpse in the swamp behind my property thanks to this guy." Imogen pointed a thumb at Ellis.

He touched his cap affirmative, took a quick sweeping glance about the bar. "What do you know about the folks that have been hanging out around here lately?"

"Who are you?" Francesca asked.

"This is Ellis," Imogen said.

"You look familiar," Francesca said. "You visit these parts often?"

"No," Ellis said, briefly hiding his face behind a mouthful of pint-glass. "I probably would have remembered that."

"So, what brings you guys out here?"

"The Jabberhouse," Imogen said. "Know anything about it?"

"The Jabberhouse?" Francesca leaned in and lowered her voice. "What are you messing about with that shit for, Im? You've noticed the agents crawling around this place, yeah?" She stepped away from them. "You left the Association, right? You're not still working for them, are you?"

"Of course not, Chess. Never again. So, can you help us out?"

"Why do you want to know?"

"They tried to kill me. If it weren't for Ellis I might be dead. He told me about them looking for the Jabberhouse, and why. We want to make sure they don't find it."

"All right. Shit, Imogen, don't go get yourself killed. What do you know already? And what do you want to know?"

"We've heard that the Jabberhouse is in the Black Widow Rainforest."

"Yeah, it's a bit of an urban legend around here."

" And that it's near the Taipan river. Could be close to Cottonmouth Valley."

"Who'd you hear that from?"

"Ellis has a guy. From the Architects. Brother Joshua."

"Don't know him. Heard a few things about the Architects though. Yeah, I know there are agents patrolling the rainforest at the moment. I'm pretty sure they've got some patrolling Cottonmouth Valley. Got any other leads?"

"That's all we've got right now," Imogen said. "Have you got anything else for us?"

"Don't go there?"

"We have to," Ellis said.

"Then don't die. Come and see me in Redback when you're done and maybe we can have a proper catch up."

"Come help us, Chess," Imogen said. "They're planning on restarting the Davinson project."

Francesca sighed. "You see a death wish on my head? We can go down to Redback together. I could put you up for the night, and you can borrow some of my gear. Not sure how much good it'll do against a Jabberhouse. But that's as far as I'm willing to go."

"Thanks Chess. When this is all done you've got to let

me take you out for a drink or dinner or something. So we can catch up properly."

"Sure thing, Sugar. I'd like that."

9
BLACK WIDOW VICTIMS

Imogen, Ellis and Francesca took Sonica to Redback. Beyond the small town, the rainforest stretched on forever. It was almost evening, and the trees were deep blue or black. The town itself was a cluster of little brick houses, small shops, and a port crammed with fishing boats. They went through town, following Francesca's directions to head right through. Her place was up around the little cliffs just beyond town, overlooking Flathead Bay. With warm yellow lanterns swinging on the porch, Sonica climbed the hill to Francesca's house.

To the place where her house used to be.

In its place: ashes. A door propped against a metal chair. A note pinned to the door.

Francesca leaped from the still moving house, hurdled the broken gate, pulled the note off the door and flung the door to the ground. Sonica sat down and Imogen and Ellis waited quietly while Francesca read the note in silence.

After a couple of minutes she turned the page over, looking for more, but that was it. She turned around slowly and looked up at Imogen.

"What is it?" Imogen asked.

"I have to go."

"Are you going to be okay?"

Francesca nodded. "This guy," she shook the note in her fist. "When I left the Association five years ago. Because of the incident with my parents..."

"Yeah, it was all over the news. I'm sorry, Chess."

"Why didn't you come to the funeral? I needed you, Im."

"I know. I just... I couldn't do it. I couldn't deal with everything back then."

"How do you think I felt?"

"I had already left the Association at the time. I didn't want you thinking I was soft. We made plans to fix the world, and I thought you'd think I failed. While, you know, while your parents stuck it through to the end."

"It's not your fault. Even back then I knew you had your reasons for leaving. It was this guy," she shook the note again. "He was responsible for it. I need to finish things with him."

Imogen nodded.

"You got any shovels?" Francesca asked. "I'll crack open my secret stash so you can help yourselves and I can get out of here."

Imogen and Ellis took the road to the Black Widow Rainforest. The house was filled with foundation bombs, demolition cannons, cerebral enhancers, cerebral disruptors, laser-guided house hunting droids. Francesca had seen this war coming.

They hadn't seen another person on this path. Up close, the rainforest was even taller, yet the path was only toothpick thin. Barely a couple of miles down the path, there were mushrooms the size of trees and trees the size of mountains. If there were mountains here, they would likely be the size of planets.

Spiders took on the size, shape, and aggressive manner of wild bears. Big furry arachnids hanging from industrial webs, red eyes staring at the intrusive house, acid breath slobbering to the rainforest floor below. Bird calls sounded like dragons roaring, and insects looked like dinosaurs. The great archaic monsters of old. Further in, and everything got bigger and darker, and the moonlight only made it to the rainforest floor in scant patches.

Imogen turned the light up on the lanterns, expanding a warm orange glow around their immediate surroundings. The light fell on a blue and red lizard fighting a giant gray owl over a dragonfly carcass that was bigger than Imogen. Tongues, beaks, claws and talons flashed with ferocity.

They followed the path straight up to the Taipan River. The river went on to run a fair way through the rainforest before reaching Cottonmouth Valley.

Imogen turned the porch lights off when the morning sunlight shone through the rainforest canopy into a clearing. Everywhere there was moss and fungi and holes with nests cut into trees and earth and rock, and all up the trees were the twisted shapes of dead sprites, faces protruding from the knotted branches, or hanging from vines. The forest their eternal prisons. Their punishment for trying to burn the forest down.

Ellis showed Imogen the map, and how far they'd come in the night. They gave Sonica a moment to rest while they wandered about the clearing. Ellis walked up to a Black Widow tree. It was all fruit and tree, branches shooting up high until gravity brought them down. Dripping with fruit shaped like dark purple rain drops. He pulled a piece of fruit from a low hanging branch and tossed it to Imogen. It had a tough, bitter skin, but the flesh was soft and sweet and blue. Juice dribbled down their chins. After about half a dozen pieces of fruit, their faces looked like they'd been feasting on demons or goliath spiders. They tossed their seeds between trees into the dense forest.

Something rustled in the branches. Then something snapped. Then something leaped from the forest and landed on Sonica. It had eight legs, red and black stripes, and a red front door. It was about four feet tall with limbs hellbent on tearing Sonica to pieces. A pygmy house. Another three leaped from the trees. Sonica reared up and tried to fling them off. No luck.

"Get off, you bastards!" Imogen yelled.

She ran towards Sonica to fight them off, but Ellis grabbed her around the waist and held her back.

"Let me go," she said. "Sonica!" She kicked and screamed and tugged free from Ellis. The pygmy houses ripped part of the roof off and a couple crawled inside while the rest of them proceeded to destroy her from the outside. Imogen ran across the clearing and latched her lightning cannon to her arm. Her wrist shook as she lifted it up to shoot down the pygmy houses. The pygmies wailed like banshees. One crawled under Sonica and slashed at its legs and underbelly. Imogen's whole body trembled. She couldn't aim straight, she couldn't see clearly, she couldn't think properly.

"Bastards!" she screamed and set the cannon to scorch. She fired a charge of violent red electricity at the pygmy houses and missed. She left a large black smouldering hole in a tree off to the side, smoke pouring out from it, the wood around it curling and blistering. The pygmy house under Sonica busted up a hole in the floor, and with it a series of water pipes.

Sonica dropped down on the pygmy house, turning it to splinters before shakily getting back up. Imogen fired again and shot down the pygmy house currently ripping into her lounge room. The shot went right through it, leaving a glowing orange hole in the creature, before it fell to the ground and burst into flames.

Ellis came up behind Imogen and rested his hand on her shoulder. "Imogen, be careful. We don't want these guys coming after us."

She shook her head and fired her cannon again. Missed.

"And you've got to watch it you don't set the whole rainforest on fire," Ellis said.

"Where the fuck's your cannon?" Imogen replied and aimed at the pygmy houses on the second story. The flaming pygmy house on the ground had burned out into a hollow box of ash.

"Inside," Ellis said.

"Go get it," she said.

"I can't," he said. "I'm sorry."

"I don't care." She aimed her cannon at Ellis. "Just make it stop, okay?"

"I'm sorry," he said. "There's not much we can do."

Tears fell freely, flowing over her chin and down her neck. "What do you know? What the fuck do you know?" She aimed the cannon back at the pygmy houses and fired. She fired again. And again. She fired.

The pygmy houses dropped off, burning, bits of Sonica still in their savage claws. More came and she fired at them too. They leaped off Sonica and came at her and Ellis, thrashing and growling and turning to flame and ash. She fell to her knees sobbing, and the pygmy houses burst into flames around the clearing. A pygmy house burst down the front door and leaped at Imogen. Its spiral roof was pushing against her chest when a burning blue hole tore through it. The flames rose and spread from the pygmy houses on to Sonica, starting with the porch.

"I'm sorry, Imogen," Ellis said.

"No," she said. "Fuck this." She ran up to Sonica and went in under her foundations, disappearing through the hole the crumbled pygmy house had made. More shots were fired, scorch beams bursting from the inside out. A lightning cannon came flying through the kitchen window, followed by a bulging burlap sack.

"Imogen!" Ellis called out. "What the fuck are you doing? Get out of there!"

The roof was beginning to cave in. The flames were spreading. Through the front room window, Imogen saw the hands of a pygmy house snatch her spider-bear off the porch, head on fire, and rip it to shreds. The oranges and reds and yellows of the fire gave way to cold shadows. The house fell down and the walls and roof began to sink. Clouds of black smoke obscured Imogen's vision and the pounding of her heartbeat in her ears drowned out all noise. Like being underwater.

Then, a sizzling green beam cut through the smoke and the silence. A section of wall slid away. Light poured in. And with it, fresh oxygen. For the lungs, but also for the flames.

"Imogen," Ellis said. "Get yourself out of there. Follow my voice."

She stumbled over the spent wall and tumbled onto the warm ground covered in ash and she stopped moving. Ellis sat down beside Imogen and patted her back, and Sonica burned to ashes.

Imogen gradually got to her feet, and she walked over to the pile of burnt house and sifted through the debris, returning with the charred brass doorknob in her ash-stained hands. Black smears up her arms and on her face and hair and clothes. "Let's go," she said. "Do you still have the map?"

Ellis nodded. He picked up the burlap sack filled with their gifts from Francesca and followed Imogen out of the clearing.

10
THE IMP

They followed the path and the map until their senses took over, following the rushing river sounds and the dampness in the air and the greener growth that flourished closer to the river. Then they were washing their hands and faces in the river and sucking down water. Imogen washed away the ash from her skin and the ash that had stuck to her face and dunked her hair in the water and turned it murky gray. She kept her head underwater and scrubbed it all away. Then she dipped Sonica's doorknob into the stream and shined it up with her shirt.

"You okay?" Ellis asked.

"Yeah," she said. She stuck the doorknob in her pocket and zipped it up safe. She followed Ellis down the river.

"What do you think the Jabberhouse looks like?"

"I hear it's like nothing you've ever seen before," Ellis said. "Beautiful. So old and majestic and huge. And terrifying. Like nothing you've ever seen before. What do you think?"

"I don't know. I just hope we can control it."

"What then? If you can control all that power, what follows?"

"It's not the power I'm worried about. I think it's more dangerous to have an uncontrollable monster than a controllable one in the wrong hands."

"Better us than the Association, yeah?"

Imogen shrugged. "Ideally, we make it so no one can have that power."

They walked along the river all day, stopping occasionally to eat fruit from the trees. As the sun went down they built a little camp, starting a fire with two rocks and a large sunburst fire ant. They caught and cooked and ate a goliath tarantula the size of a chicken. They buried the scraps and sat on the riverbank. Ellis lay down on the grass and Imogen dipped her feet in the water.

A body floated down the river. It was a man in a beige shirt and shorts, dark brown hair, floating face-down along the river, the firelight playing off his body. Its hand brushed Imogen's leg and she kicked at it and jumped out of the water. Ellis got up and ran down the river after it, but it shrank into the darkness before he could get close. He came back to Imogen crouched by the fire, shaking. He sat down by the river and watched the water flow past, waiting to see if anyone else would float past.

"Do you think it could have been the pygmies?" Imogen asked.

"Maybe." Ellis said.

"Do you think it could have been the Association?"

"Could be. I don't know. It could be any number of things."

"Do you think they'll come find us?"

"I doubt it. I don't think they know we're here. We'll be fine."

"Yeah."

Imogen stared into the fire, feeling the heat on her eyeballs.

"Wait long by the river and the bodies of your enemies will float by," Imogen said.

"What was that?"

"Just something I remember reading on a wall when I was little."

"Sounds like something brother Joshua would say."

Imogen shrugged. "I don't feel like staying here."

"It's too dark out to keep wandering upstream."

"We've got fire."

"We need rest."

"I can't sleep. What if someone's watching us? What if

they're waiting for us to go to sleep?"

"That body looked pretty bloated. It had probably been floating downstream for a while."

"Fine. You sleep if you want, I'm going to look around for a bit."

Ellis sighed. "Okay. Let's go. We should stick together."

"Okay. Whatever."

With a flashlight each, they followed the river silently until the scent of rotting meat caught them. A little river of red wove through the grass, overflowing from a blood pond at the base of a giant mushroom. All down the stem there were the streams tracked like veins. Closer, by the torchlight, a man's face reflected in the pond. He was skinless and pinned to the underside of the mushroom's cap, yellow eyes popping, flesh dripping and rotting and infested with cowfly larvae.

Choking on the stench, they backed away fast. It might have been the larvae, or maybe the torchlight on his raw flesh, but the body seemed to be shivering, crawling. At a distance, Imogen leaned against a tree and closed her eyes and took a deep breath of fresh air. She was unsure what was worse, seeing bodies like *that* or sleeping oblivious in the forest while all that shit happened around them, regardless. And the forest transformed. Everything became a potential predator. A howl. A whistle in the wind. A bird call. Footsteps and rustling and twigs snapping. The things that could kill Imogen and Ellis in an instant. A few hundred yards down the river, a family of huntsmen spiders feasted on a woman's corpse sprawled on the ground. A trail of blood disappearing into the dense scrub.

This was a brutal, merciless place. It was a wild, grotesque organism. Everything within the rainforest did what it could to survive, and through that, the rainforest had thrived for thousands of years. Ahead, in a tree reaching over the river, there was a little white glow. A series of high tweets piercing the darkness. Tiny screams that absorbed into the forest and vanished, then repeated, and vanished again.

A body plunged into the river and the white glow scattered into many tiny lights. The body bobbed up in the river and floated past, the torchlight just barely catching the bloody, wet lump before it was swallowed by the darkness downstream. The scattered lights darted about, screeching frequently. They grew larger as they came closer and their light took a more distinct form.

They were silver canaries, glowing from within, chirping and watching the house hunters follow the river. They sat on branches up ahead, and when Imogen and Ellis reached them, they flew further down the river and waited. It was as though the canaries were guiding them like a prophetic star through the rainforest, down the trail by the river that seemed to go back in time. The trees were even taller, and the dead sprites buried within them were shaped like giants and dragons and minotaurs and great bearded rainforest gods. All trapped and dead and fossilised in what can only be imagined as thousands of years of battles over the Black Widow. Some trees even had stories etched into them of shapes that were now like clouds. They could look like anything from elephants to children to chairs to planes to celebrities. If only the etchings could speak for themselves, the stories they'd tell.

Along the treetops, there were the long-haired tree-houses of old. Born of the forest, they grew into their surroundings, grew from the rudimentary materials to be— at times—quite elaborate. And some of them moved from tree to tree, some just grew around one tree or between a few trees and just hung there. But they were all alive and humming with a beautiful natural energy. The rainforest floor here was littered with the splinters and skeletons of the tree-houses that had died and dropped off, and there were now dragon beetles and vampire moles and gold-breasted bilbies living in these pre-built nests.

Up ahead, a tree had fallen over across the river, and a baby tree-house was walking across it, taking its steps slowly and carefully. It jumped off the end, looked across at Imogen and Ellis, and ran off.

The canaries flew over the river by the fallen tree and waited.

The house hunters climbed across the river, and the

canaries flew off through the trees, leading them away from the river. They pushed branches aside and tugged at vines and swept cobwebs from out of their faces, following these darting orbs of silver light. Still carrying their torches burned down to their embers, their light didn't stretch much past the next tree. Then there was not much point carrying them at all. As long as the birds were visible up ahead, they could search blindly through their immediate surroundings.

The canaries flew out along a rocky ledge that dropped down into Cottonmouth Valley. They wandered along the ledge for a little while before dipping into the valley. They perched on the rock face part-way down the ledge and waited for Imogen and Ellis to turn their backs to the valley, grip the hard ground at their feet, and start climbing down.

Imogen tossed the bag down, then lowered one foot, and the other. Then a boulder slammed into the ledge. The birds scattered and Imogen and Ellis came tumbling down, catching scrapes and bruises as they went.

"Imogen. Where are you? Are you okay?" Ellis called out.

"Yeah, I'm fine. I'm over here."

The boulder that knocked them down rolled back into the valley, and Imogen and Ellis saw them. The stone temples running through the valley throwing trees and boulders at each other and crashing into each other and destroying everything. They sounded like thunder and the resulting collisions left a fine powder hanging in the air.

Imogen walked gingerly up to Ellis and said, "What now? Those things will crush us in no time flat."

"We've been following those canaries, yeah? Maybe they'll show us a safe passage through the valley."

"Or maybe they'll lure us into a trap and dump us in the river like that other body back there."

Ellis shrugged. "What else is there to do? Play demolition derby with the temples?" He slung the burlap sack over his shoulder and started wandering off after the flock of silver canaries ahead.

"Hurry up, Imogen," Ellis said. "I think they're getting away from us."

In the distance, the thunder of warring stone temples carried through the valley.

They came to a tall cliff with a wide cave.

The silver canaries flew inside.

"Keep following them?" Ellis asked.

Imogen shrugged then nodded.

They could see down a long passage lit with torches. Sitting on a rock just inside the entrance was a very small man with dark orange skin and dragonfly wings. A faery or an imp, or something.

"Whoa there," he said. "You don't want to go in there."

"Why not?" Ellis asked.

"That's the labyrinth, that is. You go in there, you get lost. You don't ever get found." He grinned and flew up to face Ellis. "So . . . get lost."

"Why? What's in there?"

"Ain't nothing in there worth your time, sir."

"Any more temples we should watch out for?"

"Yeah, probably," the imp said. "But you go in there, you're probably not coming back. I've seen many people come through here. Never any coming back."

"Do you think they might be coming out the other side?" Imogen asked.

"Don't be a wise ass. You want me to hand out maps of the labyrinth to all the visitors? You want me to impart my sacred wisdom onto you or something? Beat it, chumps."

"Damn pixie asshole." Ellis grabbed the imp and brought it close to his face. "Quit fucking around with us. This is a labyrinth, yeah? Tell me, when did the last people come through here?"

"A labyrinth, that's what I said. Yeah, the last people that came through here you've already seen. Taking a dip in the river," the imp cackled. "The rainforest holds no mercy for the humans. Mark my words: You will not leave here alive." The imp bit down on Ellis' hand and flew off.

"Fucker!" Ellis sucked the bite then wiped it on his sleeve. He entered the labyrinth and turned to Imogen. "You coming or what?"

11
THE JABBERWOCK

They stopped at the first fork in the path.

"If I were a Jabberhouse," Ellis said, "A labyrinth would be a good place to hide my cerebrum. Left or right?"

"You can't use logic with these things," Imogen said, and went left.

"Wait up. Shouldn't we leave some sort of marking to find our way back?"

"Don't you read books? Everyone jumps on that idea but they wind up lost anyway. They lose their markers or they start seeing markers where there are none. They get confused. It just gets them more lost than they would be with no markings at all." Imogen disappeared around the corner.

She followed the maze and Ellis followed her, and no more sound passed between them but footsteps. Further in, the air became colder and tighter. The lights guiding them put out only small spheres of wasted heat. It must have been close to three hours into the labyrinth when they came across the first skeleton resting against the wall.

"Do you think this guy died of hunger or something got him?" Ellis asked.

Imogen shrugged. "Does it matter? It's the maze that got to him."

"Yeah."

"Hey," Imogen said. "There's something up ahead."

There was a stream of sunlight coming from a passageway. A staircase up to the outside. A cage around them along a massive plateau. The edges of the valley off in the distance. The thunder of stone temples. The plateau was covered in dozens, maybe hundreds, of lookout cages. The nearest one to them had a skeleton in it, arms hanging through the gaps, head resting against the cage.

"Can you see anything?" Ellis asked.

"Like what?"

"Like anything. Some sort of reference point so we're not just going blindly from lookout to lookout."

"You clearly haven't read any books. Reference points are only here to trick us. We'd only end up trying to force our way in one direction instead of following the flow of the maze. That's where all the traps and dead-ends are." Imogen went back downstairs. "You can't hope to figure out a maze like this with basic tricks."

Ellis returned to following Imogen in silence.

The ground trembled and little bits of dust and rubble fell from the roof and walls.

"This way," Imogen said, and set off running down a passageway that had torches fallen on the ground and gone out.

"How can you be so sure?" Ellis said. "I think we need to find another lookout."

"This way!" Imogen called over her shoulder. She disappeared around the corner at the end of the passage up ahead. the labyrinth rumbled with greater aggression.

"Wait up," Ellis called out. He ran after her but his foot slipped on something squishy on the ground and he fell. It was like a water bed: unstable, and displaced the moment he stepped on it. But it wasn't something on the ground, it was *in* the ground. Embedded into the earth. A giant eye, blinking and weeping and red and staring at him. He got up and ran after Imogen, following the corner to another lookout, where Imogen waited for him.

"Back there," Ellis panted, "in the ground, an eye. A big eye in the ground. Did you see it?"

"Shh," Imogen said. "We're moving."

"What?"

"We're moving. This labyrinth. It's alive. Watch the valley over there." Imogen pointed. "The trees. We're definitely moving."

The trees in the distance appeared to shrink into themselves.

"It's standing up," she said. "What's that hole over there? Is that the middle of the maze?" She returned downstairs and disappeared back into the labyrinth.

While the labyrinth walked steadily north, gaining height and speed, Imogen and Ellis walked to its middle. There were eyes opening on the walls and roof and floor. They watched Imogen and Ellis pull torches from the wall and walk past.

The passages seemed to expand and contract a little like they were controlling air flow. Some sections periodically opened and closed. Stone slamming on stone and snapping back like it was rubber.

They came out of one passage into a wide room filled with plants and trees that flickered with light instead of fruit and flowers and leaves, and filled the room with the scent of peaches and roses and eucalyptus. The plants grew from little islands of red soil that were surrounded by a black liquid sea. Along the walls, eyes watched them. Imogen went out into the sea, knee deep. Ellis followed. In the centre of the room, a tree spiralled up like a staircase, disappearing into a hole in the roof.

"Do you think we could drink this water?" Imogen said.

"I wouldn't."

"I'm so thirsty."

"I know. Me too."

Ellis sat down on the red island in the middle of the room while Imogen climbed the tree.

"What's up there? Can you see?"

"It's… I don't know," Imogen said. She climbed the branches, grabbing on to the formations of light and pulling herself up. She put her head through the hole in the roof and saw everything. She saw her headless body standing in the tree from eighty different angles. She saw the floor, walls, and ceiling of every part of the tunnel. And the eyes staring at each other. She must have seen a thousand things. The eyes of the labyrinth. And there must have been at least a dozen more rooms like this one, with house-shaped plants, and plant-shaped animals, and nests of mole-spiders, wattle-wasps, and a room that gazed up at a big hole in the roof, the sky moving past, a statue in the middle. Flashes of simultaneous images, hundreds of skeletons littered about, lost and alone, mostly human, some animals, some beasts like nothing Imogen had ever seen. She screamed and tugged her head from the hole.

"Are you alright?" Ellis asked.

"I know where to go," she replied, climbing down and wandering off as if being pulled by an invisible thread.

They stared up at the brass statue of a monster, with jaws that bite and claws that snatch, eyes of flame and a plaque that read: *THE JABBERWOCK*. On either side of the statue were staircases going beneath the ground.

Imogen and Ellis entered the Jabberhouse. The walls were made out of a collage of stone, timber, and a soft, fleshy material, and had become overgrown with vines and moss, and dead sprites had grown into the building, the outlines of their bodies etched into the walls. Now that it was alive again, it seemed as though everything inside the Jabberhouse had come to life too. The trapped sprites turned their heads as Imogen and Ellis went past. Vines snaked out across the walls. Leaves spread over the floor like carpet, muffling their footsteps, and possibly muffling the footsteps of anything else out to get them.

It felt like imps were following them. Or maybe it was the strange candlelight playing tricks on the walls. There were narrow corridors and wide halls and many, many bedrooms and bathrooms and dining rooms and spaces that just didn't seem to end. Everything seemed to be alive; crawling or breathing or shrinking and expanding, changing from one moment to the next. Yes, this building had definitely been brought back from the dead. It would follow that the people who resurrected this monster had to be somewhere inside.

Outside, the tree-houses, pygmy houses and stone temples came from the rainforest and followed the Jabberhouse as it knocked over trees, and crushed the plants and animals on the rainforest floor below.

Imogen and Ellis found themselves in a large dance hall where the entire east wall was glass, and they could see the pygmy houses piggy-backing on the tree-houses as they swung and leaped their way from the trees to latch on to the Jabberhouse wall. They could see part of the outer wall through the window, covered in houses holding on by rough rock knobs and handles that naturally formed out of the wall.

In the dance hall, there was a swamp growing from the floor, vines hanging from the ceiling, and a group of humanoid sprites reanimated and fighting a dragon-sprite. One sprite sat on the shoulders of a tree golem as it swung a massive granite sledgehammer. The dragon-sprite leapt on the attacking sprites and tore at them and stabbed with its overgrown horns. Ellis dropped a foundation bomb on the dragon-sprite and he and Imogen climbed the stairs to the balcony path that led to the nearest exit.

They followed a long hallway to a large wooden door.

"This is it," Imogen said. "I think. It feels like the place."

"Didn't you see this back in the labyrinth?"

Imogen shrugged. "It was mostly just the maze. I mean, I'm sure this part of the building was there too. It just wasn't really clear."

"So, what's inside?"

"There are five, maybe six guys from the Assocation."

"All right. We can do this." Ellis pulled out his lightning cannon and indicated Imogen to do the same. "Ready to destroy this place, yeah?"

Imogen opened the door to a series of lightning cannons aimed at her. The room was tall, with a window like a giant eye. A giant throne faced the window with spider web patterns and long thin legs sticking out and a spider's head perched on top. A man sat in the throne, controlling the Jabberhouse as it crushed over the rainforest.

"Drop your cannons," a woman said. "Who are you, and what are you doing here?"

"We came down through the labyrinth," Imogen said, lowering her cannon.

"You don't just casually wander through the Black fucking Widow Rainforest. Who are you? What are you doing here?"

"Settle down, Adeline," the man on the throne said. He stood up, not much taller. He had large, black compound eyes on white skin, a little black goatee that looked like a beetle's shell. Imogen sensed the power of the Jabberhouse, its cerebrum, was contained in the spider throne.

The man looked at Imogen, then at Ellis, then he grinned. "Ellis! Lovely to see you. How's your dear brother doing these days?"

"He's dead, Leroy," Ellis said.

"Oh. Well I guess you're here to finish off what he started, yeah? Going to try to sabotage the new world order again?" Leroy walked up to Ellis and punched his arm. "We're looking at the bigger picture here. This world is going to become a very exciting, very prosperous place in the near future. You're shooting yourself in the foot, Ellis. This building. This right here. The cerebrum of the Jabberhouse is powerful enough to communicate with other buildings. We can monitor and control entire cities from right here. Pull them apart and rebuild them bigger and better. We can keep everything in order and shut down anything that tries to interfere. Now, I can't have you running around here stirring shit up, so I'm going to lock you away until our job is done, ok? When we're finished, I'll take you out and show you all the progress we've made. You'll come back round. It'll be like the good old days, how does that sound?"

Ellis shrugged.

"Fine. Whatever. Lock them up." Leroy returned to his throne, and Ellis and Imogen were dragged out.

Imogen and Ellis sat on the floor in a room with no windows and one door. One lit candle in the center of the room.

"What happens now?" Imogen said. The question echoed a few times around the room before it found a response.

"We give up. They tear the city apart. They destroy your home town. They build their dream cities and towns. They farm houses and raise them to slaughter. Can't do nothing now."

The room felt damp, like underground caves formed over thousands of years from cold stone and trickling streams. Here, there was cold stone and dim candlelight.

"What sort of answer is that?" Imogen said. "I thought you were better than that. You're the guy who broke out of jail, wrestled a convenience store, and hijacked my house. And you're giving up?"

"Yeah. That jail break took me fifteen fucking years. Why don't you think of something?"

"What else is there to do?" She ran her fingers through her hair. "So how did you do it? How'd you escape? Is there nothing we can use that'll help us here?" She stood up and walked about the room, feeling her hands along the walls for a secret door or a loose brick or a crack or something.

"No," Ellis said, sighing and dumping his head into his hands. "The thing about my break was that—as far as everyone was concerned—it never happened. Before I broke out there was one person in my cell. After, there was one person in my cell." He took off his cap and squeezed it in his hands. "My brother." He shrugged. "Identical twin."

Imogen sat down and stared at Ellis.

"It was the one compassionate thing he ever did for me. We never really got along with each other. It's like we were just on two different wavelengths. Then I went to jail and he couldn't figure out why. I was the good kid. The role model. He was the one that was always wandering off and no one would hear from him for months at a time. Sometimes it was like I hardly had a brother at all.

"Then he visited me in jail. Once a month for fifteen years. And we would just talk. About anything. And him being there, it diffused the tension between us. All those years thinking I was better than him, when he was the one who was there for me. He made me realize I was wrong.

He wanted to be there for me so that I'd have a chance to correct my mistakes. And now he's gone and died on me." Ellis hugged his knees. His eyes were tearing up and shiny in the candlelight. "Then he started talking of breaking me out. And each time he came to see me it was to work on the escape plan. And then," Ellis pulled out a handkerchief and blew his nose.

"Then he breaks in with a machine he invented. Apparently while I was making my career, he was busy being quite the mechanic. So this machine – he called it the Juggernaut – smashed its way into the cell block. It smashed in and did its thing. In the chaos, we swapped and I escaped. They did the math and examined the damage and left it at that." He stared into the flame. "Ellis was my brother's name. He's dead, but legally I'm dead."

"Who are you?" Imogen asked.

"Charles Davinson."

12

RETURN TO HUNTSMAN CITY

"Ellis, you're amazing," Imogen said.

"Well," he said. "I had to break into *your* place." His laugh was dry.

"And all the shit you did for the Association," she said. "You can't just forget that."

They sat staring at the candle. Ellis had formed a weak connection between the room and the cerebrum through the candle. It burned brighter.

"Leroy won't feel this, will he?" Imogen said.

Ellis shook his head. "I don't think so."

The room warmed up a little. Wax dripped down the candle and burned Ellis' hand, beads of hot wax running over the back of his hand and over his knuckles.

"And you think this room will just let us out?" Imogen said.

"Maybe. It's a nice room. I think it likes me." He got up—wax dripping to the floor—and rubbed his palm on the wall. In that small patch, a little tuft of moss began to grow. "I think it's working," he said. He worked his way along the wall, bringing the room to life. Little plants sprouted from the cracks and opened up little light-flowers that wreathed around and spiralled up to the roof, painting the walls with light and color. He brought the candle up close to a brick near the ground that looked like a face. The creeper plants wound their way towards the brick, and his eyes flicked open. His jaw cracked.

"Who are you?" the sprite said.

"We're prisoners in here. Do you know a way out?"

"I'm a prisoner, myself. I've been trapped in this wall for seven hundred years, maybe more." The man's face cracked and came loose from the surrounding bricks. He pulled his face out of the hole and stuck a hand through. "Name's Andrew."

"Ellis." He shook the outstretched hand.

"You looking for doors and windows, Ellis?"

"We're looking for a way out."

"Aren't we all?" Andrew said with a chuckle.

"What?"

"Never mind. That door's not going to budge for you."

"Why not?"

"The Jabberhouse is dead. Just because it's up and walking about, doesn't mean it's the same house as the fables. Doesn't mean it's the same house it was back when it was alive."

"So what can the Association do with it?"

"This thing is a destruction machine. The only thing it's good for is levelling cities. You want to know a way out?"

"Sure. What have you got?"

"There's a tunnel back here. You're welcome to join me if you think you can fit." Andrew slid back from the hole, face turning to shadows, eyes turning to light.

Ellis held the candle up to the hole and it appeared to melt the rock away until there was a man-sized hole they could fit through. Andrew's skin was the same color as his face, a navy blue/black that blended with the stone bricks. He wandered through the tunnel and Imogen and Ellis followed. The plants on the wall began to wilt and die the moment they entered the tunnel.

Ellis melted a little hole in the door to the hallway that took them to Leroy. There was one agent standing guard outside the room.

"We need to draw him away," Imogen said. "If we could create a diversion, we could probably steal his cannon too."

Ellis nodded.

"I'll do it," Andrew said. "You guys wait over there." He

pointed to the corner behind the door.

Andrew threw the door open and hollered down the hall. He ducked as cannon fire shot over his head. "Good luck," he said, then ran off, disappearing into another room.

Ellis greeted the agent with a candlestick to the face. Imogen slammed the door shut and grabbed him by the arm and tugged at his canon. A shot went through the roof. Plaster and bits of plant rained down on them, and Imogen popped the canon off. She hit the agent with a light stun to the chest. Through the hole in the door, she watched more agents come out into the hall.

"Can you make this hole a bit bigger?" she asked Ellis.

He showed her his broken candle and shrugged, the wax had dried his hand into a fist.

"I guess we just wait for them," she said.

The door opened again and an agent came through. Imogen slammed it shut and stunned him. Ellis took his canon.

"Mark," a voice said. Adeline. "Are they out there?"

No response.

"Mark? We're coming through."

Imogen and Ellis stepped back from the door and aimed their cannons at it. A red beam fired a hole through the door, taking Imogen's right arm with it. She cried out and held her canon arm to the cauterized stump where her other arm used to be. Ellis knocked his canon up a setting and returned fire through the enlarged hole in the door. Imogen dropped to her knees.

"Are you okay, Imogen?" Ellis said, shooting the agent that pushed the door open. He stood in front of her and lined up the agents and one, two, three, shot them down. "Are you okay? Talk to me."

"Hm?" she said. Her face was pale and some of her hair was singed off and some of it had melted. "What's that smell?"

Ellis lifted her back onto her feet. "You'll be okay," he said. "We've almost got him." He wrapped his arm around Imogen, the broken candle sticking into her side while her stump-arm squished against his shoulder. Forest sprites entered the hall and came at Imogen and Ellis, and Ellis shot them down. A golem ripped off bits of wall and floor and threw them at Imogen and Ellis. Again, Ellis shot it down, scattering the floor with rubble. Imogen raised her lightning cannon and helped turn the hall into the third world.

It felt like her nerves were on fire, but she just wiped her hair out of her face and went with Ellis to go stop Leroy.

The wall came crashing down as Leroy burst through on his throne. Long, thin spider legs carrying him out. Lightning cannons fixed to the throne's arms.

"That's enough!" he said, and fired his cannons at Imogen and Ellis.

They ducked and rolled out of the way and Ellis fired his cannon blindly in Leroy's direction. He missed. Imogen crouched and ran and burned off three of his throne's legs. It tilted forward and Leroy came close to sliding out onto the floor. Ellis took another shot and destroyed Leroy's left cannon. He took aim at the right one, but a sprite came from the floor and pulled Ellis to ground. Another sprite leaped from the wall and tackled Imogen down. More emerged and crowded around them. Then a minotaur sprite fell from the ceiling and landed on Leroy, crushing him.

Ellis wrestled the sprites off him and turned his cannon to the sprites attacking Imogen. He was hot and sweaty and blood was dribbling down his face and his body was aching. And his cannon was burning up the moisture in the air and he felt dizzy and sick and he felt like he was going to pass out. He couldn't see Imogen moving. He could barely see her at all.

The minotaur slugged him across the head with a massive stone hammer and he fell to the ground, limp. The last image he saw was Imogen's body rising from the mass of sprites with a massive cockroach-sprite gripping her around the neck. She slammed her back against the wall, crushing the sprite. Its fingers loosened on her neck and she blasted its hands with her cannon. The nerves on her neck tingled and stung from the heat, and the sprite fell back. She turned around and kicked it and fired her cannon into its chest and head. Her nose was broken and bleeding. Her cheek was swollen and purple. But she was the one-armed fury. She lined the sprites up in her cannon and took them down. The minotaur charged at her, hammer mid-swing, and she took off its head. Big hulking humanoid-ox body sliding to a rest at her feet.

The sprites were all gone, and Imogen ran over to Ellis and rolled him onto his side.

She slapped his face. "Wake up, Ellis. Wake up, we're here."

He opened his eyes a crack and said, "We made it. See, I told you we would."

"Come on," she said. "Get up. It's not over, yet." She helped him to his feet, pulling with her one good arm.

They hobbled over to the throne and slid Leroy's mangled body from the seat.

"Fuck your new world order," Ellis said to Leroy on the ground. "You had it all wrong." He leaned against the throne, holding his head. "The Association was founded on the idea that we needed to look out for these creatures. The Jabberhouse changes *nothing*. It won't fix anything. Let it rest, Leroy. The Davinson project was a failure. I wish I'd never started it."

"Charles," Leroy croaked. "This is your... failure." He wheezed, like his ribcage had been turned into an accordion.

"Charles is dead. I'm just here to try to clean up his mess."

"Too late, Charles. Too... late."

"Ellis," Imogen said. "Look at this." She pointed through the hole in the wall at the window.

The city came up on the horizon, thick black smokestacks rising into the sky. The skyline was scorched with flames and toxic fog, sky-scrapers ripping each other to pieces, tumbling down on entire city blocks while other buildings fled.

"Tell me about the revivification cannon," Ellis said. "How many does the Association have?"

"Just the one," Leroy sighed.

"Where is it?"

Leroy took a deep, wheezing breath, body shaking like mad.

"Where is it?"

He took another deep, painful breath. "It's... in there." He pointed at the hole in the wall.

"Hey Ellis," Imogen said. "What's that big thing coming from the north?"

13

THE BATTLE OF HAMMERHEAD CASTLE

A castle walked into Huntsman City.

"What is that?" Imogen asked.

"Impossible," Ellis said.

"What?"

"Hammerhead Castle. Another building from the old times. I thought they were all extinct." Ellis grabbed Leroy up off the ground. "How many revivification canons are there?"

Wheeze.

"What does it matter?" Imogen said. "What can we do about the castle?"

Hammerhead Castle tore through the city, bringing with it an army of red goliath tarantula walkers.

"Take a seat, Imogen. We need you to take it down."

"You think I can?" she said.

Ellis nodded.

She sat down on the throne and thousands of little sparks reached out and grabbed her and pulled her into the throne holding her there like she was stitched into the stone. Just like she saw everything in the labyrinth before, she felt everything now. The dozens of legs powering this beast. The sprites in all the rooms.

The tree-houses and the pygmy houses hanging on to the Jabberhouse walls. They were all connected and waiting for her. The rush to her brain of feeling and knowing so many things, to have so much power. Imogen looked through the giant eye-shaped window. The castle and the walkers. The tree-houses and pygmy houses dropped from her walls and ran with stone temples through the sprawling suburbs with urgency and deliberation. The Jabberhouse came down into the city, charging right towards Hammerhead Castle.

They clashed in the city center towering over apartment complexes and brushing up against skyscrapers that reached far higher into the sky than either giant. The Jabberhouse pushed up against Hammerhead Castle, and the sprites leaped over and burst their way inside the castle. Giant sparks from lightning cannons passed from Jabberhouse to Hammerhead Castle, from Hammerhead to Jabberhouse. It pushed back and ripped up the telecommunications tower with its massive spire hands, wielding it like a sword, smashing the building into the Jabberhouse's side, crushing a hole in its outer wall. It stumbled aside, and the castle threw the broken pieces of tower at it. It shook the debris off and charged the castle, loosening a chunk of stone on a long vine and whipping it around at one of the castle's outermost spires. The rubble rained down on the battling goliath walkers and tree-houses and pygmy houses and stone temples.

Hammerhead Castle swung another tower at the Jabberhouse, and the Jabberhouse held up a limb to stop it. The glass shattered and the metal twisted and cut into it, and the Jabberhouse swung its stone at the castle again and took off another spire. Goliath spider walkers had begun hacking at the Jabberhouse's leg, as the pygmy houses and tree houses were ripping little chunks off the castle. It was nothing to the giant beasts. More towers crashed down on the Jabberhouse, and it whipped its stones on vine-arms down on the castle, swinging two or three at a time, smashing away at its towers and walls. Two beasts only good for destruction.

The Jabberhouse rumbled and a wide mouth opened up just beneath the giant eye window and it spoke, booming, in Imogen's voice. "People and houses of the city. Please keep out of our way! We don't want to hurt you. Please, leave the city where it is safe to do so. Do not return until we are gone."

Hammerhead Castle stabbed a tower through the Jabberhouse's mouth.

"Go," Imogen said, and whipped half a dozen large rocks through the castle's front entrance.

Hammerhead Castle stepped back and withdrew its

spire-arms. Its stones rolled and twisted and reshaped into a crouching grey dragon with a fat bulging head like a sledgehammer. A wave of electricity crawled over the creature, turning its stone-scales white, with flashes of blue and green. It whipped its tail down and tore down a row of skyscrapers. The dragon opened its mouth and a series of flying somethings came pouring out. Dragonflies.

Men sat in the saddles of the winged beasts, and swooped up over the Jabberhouse, dropping bombs. The building trembled as the labyrinth roof blew apart. Around them, a lot of houses had cleared out, with the remaining few either dead or dying. The debris rained down heavily, the goliaths and tree-houses and pygmies and stone temples still fighting each other and trying to tear down the giants at street level. Imogen backed up a bit, slinging her rocks at the dragonflies. Some of them went spiralling and crashing to the ground, and some of them backed off. Some returned to Hammerhead Castle and dropped a few bombs on the dragon. Those were her sprites hijacking the dragonflies, riding them. She felt their hands gripping the leather reins on the dragonflies, turning them back to destroy their master. And the Jabberhouse continued to rumble.

"What are you doing?" Ellis asked.

"I'm not sure. I'm not really doing anything."

The Jabberhouse was transforming on its own. It grew taller—standing on thick hind legs. It tore bits of labyrinth roof off and arranged the broken pieces over its body like armor. In the center of its chest was the light garden, the spiraling tree sticking out, an organic lightning canon direct from the Black Widow Rainforest.

The creature resembled some form of wolf-bear-bull-spider-lizard-monster, but more accurately resembled the statue in the labyrinth: the Jabberwock. The dragon leaped head first at the Jabberhouse and grappled it around the midsection, sending them both tumbling over. The Jabberhouse swiped a furious claw at the dragon's throat, missed, kicked it off, then sprang to its feet. It fired its canon, burning the dragon down its side.

"Holy shit!" Ellis said, getting to his feet.

Imogen threw her hands up. "I've got no control!"

The dragon opened its mouth and fired a blue bolt from its canon-tongue. The Jabberhouse rolled out of the way. Ellis fell over again, yet the room remained upright, rolling in balance with the Jabberhouse's motion. Imogen peeled herself from the throne.

"Hey," Ellis said, "There's something else in the sky."

It was a little bird house and a white crane-house flying towards Hammerhead Castle. The crane shot a series of fists straight through the dragon like machine-gun fire. The bird house released its silver canary, whose bird song froze the dragon in its steps, and sent it crashing to the ground.

The dragonflies swung around and started firing down upon brother Joshua and Sadie. The architects darted around the canon fire and Sadie sent a string of tiny fists back at them, shredding through wings and flesh. Brother Joshua returned his canary to its home and went flying straight for the Jabberhouse. He smashed right through the middle of the giant window, glass shattering all over the floor, and Sadie followed shortly after, with Charlotte folding into a tiger as she came through the window.

"What happened to your arm?" Joshua said.

"Lost it in a gunfight," Imogen said.

"I'm sorry," he said. "We did not know about Hammerhead Castle."

"Yeah," Ellis said. "Caught us off guard, too."

"You know who they got controlling it?"

Ellis shrugged. "Some more guys from the Association?."

"Rebels. They got them working for the Association, though. But things up north have been worse than here. They're mad. They'll stop at nothing to get a do-over on everything. They'd rather destroy everything than admit fault."

"So what do we do?" Imogen asked. "We've got no control over the Jabberhouse."

"Did you find out about that revivifying canon the Association had?" Joshua said.

"Yeah, we've got it here," Imogen said.

"Good. Now come over here. The dragon will awaken soon."

Imogen picked up the revivification canon and handed it to Joshua. He kneeled down and indicated for Imogen to do the same.

"Now, let me see…" Joshua looked over the canon then placed it on the ground. He waved Ellis to join them. "Show me your candle-hand."

Ellis held his hand out to brother Joshua, broken candle glued into it, moulded in place with dried wax.

"Fantastic," Joshua said. "Wonderful. This is exactly what I need." He slid both his hands around the wax-glued hand, slotted his fingers together forming a sphere, and squeezed. A loud crack, and Joshua pulled the candle loose, Ellis' hand stuck in the shape of holding something. Joshua picked up the cannon and held it up to Imogen's side and raised the candle to her blistered shoulder.

Hot wax dripped onto tender flesh and Imogen winced. Then, the wax went from milky white to gloss black. It grew into a ball of stone and extended down to her phantom elbow, where it moulded around the cannon and formed joints.

"It won't feel like your other arm did, but it's got to count for something. And you can't *grab* things with it. And," Joseph put the candle down, pried open a little metal plate on the canon, and leaned in, poking and shifting and pulling and adjusting its mechanics, "we don't want you bringing any more monsters to life, now. Try moving it." He snapped the plate shut.

Imogen lifted her arm, waved the cannon around, then let it drop by her side. She rubbed the stone with her hand. It was cold and rough.

"Okay, Imogen," Joshua said. "What you have now is more or less a cerebral destructor. You fire that canon at a cerebrum, you'll kill it where it stands."

Imogen nodded. "So what you're saying," she said, "Is that if I can take out Hammerhead Castle and the Jabberhouse, I can end this thing?"

Brother Joshua nodded.

"Can I borrow your bird house?"

"Hop on," he said, and patted the roof of the bird house.

"Wait," Ellis said. "You should take this with you." He

passed the sack of Francesca's weaponry to Imogen.

"Thanks," she said. She took it and sat down on the bird house. The silver canary came out and landed on Imogen and the hand came out and reached into the burlap sack. It pulled out a cerebral enhancer and stabbed the canary with it. Its claws dug into Imogen's shoulder and the bird house hovered. Then massive white wings burst from its sides, and stretched and flapped. Imogen passed the burlap sack to the bird house's hand and gripped its roof. Joshua held on to it from beneath. The bird house lifted them up and flew out the window toward the temple.

From up high, Imogen had a good view of the two archaic beasts. They soared down to ground level, where Joshua let go of the bird house and leapt through an opening in a high window on his temple.

Clinging to the bird house with one hand and one canon, Imogen flew back up toward the dragon, which had resumed attacking the Jabberhouse with everything it had, while the Jabberhouse jumped and kicked and snapped and whipped and fired its cannon like an architectural virtuoso with a death wish.

Dragonflies tried to shoot Imogen down. She zoomed away and circled around and tested out her new arm-canon. Her shot blasted right through a dragonfly, leaving a scorch mark on the dragon-castle behind it. She shot a couple more down, and pulled out the foundation bombs and scattered them over the rebel walkers on the ground. She retrieved a laser-guided house hunting droid, a machine that looks like a headless bat-monkey hybrid. She set her aim for the dragon-castle and threw the thing from the bird house. It went off flying toward the dragon's head.

The droid entered through the mouth and shot its limbs off, shooting four separate electrical charges through four separate pressure points in its head. Its jaw snapped open wide and froze in place and Imogen flew in and landed in its flat stone mouth as the temple of the architects—much smaller than the Jabberhouse and Hammerhead Castle—ran at the dragon, hammer-fist raised. It slammed down its weight on the dragon's front foot. The dragon tried to pull back, but the temple had driven a nail through its foot into the ground, and each tug of the nail sent a shock up the limb. The temple leapt around to the back foot, and Imogen disappeared into the dragon.

She walked into a skirmish of sprites and rebels, all down the hallway, fists flying and cannons firing. Tree-wizards and bear sprites and two-headed giants conquered the hall. Legends of the north. Hell bent on destruction. She ran past them, firing her cannons at anyone who came too near. In a long dining hall, there were half a dozen sprites and men fighting, a minotaur-sprite standing over an unarmed rebel, cowering in the corner.

Imogen fired her cerebral destructor at the minotaur-sprite and tore a hole through his torso.

The minotaur-sprite turned.

She fired again and took off his head. She pointed her cannon at the man. "Who's in charge here?"

"What?"

"Who's in charge? Where can I find them?"

The man pointed down the dining hall.

She went through the kitchen, empty, into the storage cupboard, where she blasted a hole in the wall into a bedroom suite. She crawled through in time to witness a red-haired hornet-man blow a sprite's head off. Green blood spattered on the walls. Bits of wooden skull fragments sliding down. Imogen fired a warning shot at the roof.

"Drop it," he said. "I've got you in my peripherals."

"Can't," Imogen said. "It's fixed to my arm." She waved her cerebral destructor at him. "You drop it." She shot her cannon through the wall right beside his face. "All these sprites trying to kill you. Trying to destroy everything. It's your own fucking fault. It won't stop until this dragon is dead. You take me to the heart of this beast and maybe we won't wind up dead under four hundred tons of debris."

He lowered his cannon.

"The last guy sent me to the fucking kitchen. Don't mess around with me."

"All right. He's in the dungeon." He led Imogen out into the hall. "What you hoping to accomplish anyway? The city's already turned to shit."

"You're not doing anything to help. What were you even trying to do?"

"It was meant to be a clean slate. Going back to square one."

"But it didn't work out that way, huh?"

"I guess not."

"There's no such thing as a clean slate."

The hornet-man shrugged.

Further into the dragon, there was a greater concentration of sprites.

There was a room that was three stories tall, with giant barbarians throwing fire at each other. Imogen and the hornet-man passed beneath the barbarians' feet without so much as a passing glance.

There was a room with trees hanging from the ceiling, ripe spiked melons fell and cracked the floor tiles.

In a room like a giant blood-red cave, there were houses grown from crystal formations, bouncing rainbows and twisted images amongst themselves and distorting the space into an open crystal maze. The houses moaned deep, hollow bottle cries and tugged at their foundations, leering at Imogen and the hornet-man. They tugged at thousands of years of formation, and they mutated the refractions of everything around them. And one small crystal house came free and leaped at the intruders. Imogen fired her cerebral destructor. It rained crystal shards down on them.

It became the beginning of a flood. More houses broke free and lunged forward. And Imogen destroyed them. And more came and she destroyed them too. The room turned into a giant hollow cavern. The floor was covered in shiny crystal shards. Imogen's body was covered in fine crystal dust that shimmered in the light.

Imogen nudged the hornet-man forward, through the cave of crystal houses, and down a flight of stairs. They entered a room that was round and lit by dim blue torches. The floor was sticky and soft with what Imogen could think of only as dragon blood. In the dungeon there was the skeleton of a dragon, roaring and flying into the walls. Blind and mad and undead. It slammed into Imogen and hornet-man and knocked them over and flew back through the dungeon.

Hornet-man got up coughing and holding his side. "All right. Now you found it. Now what?"

Imogen rolled over and pulled herself up so she was leaning against the wall. She waved her cannon-arm for hornet-man again. "Now we kill it."

The dragon pulled up and turned its head around, sniffing. It took a few steps back towards Imogen and hornet-man, and Imogen fired, rattling its bones, burning it to ash.

Imogen and hornet-man tumbled as Hammerhead Castle crashed into the ground.

EPILOGUE

The screen reads: *Heston Blake, President of the House Hunter Association.* The man on the screen has slick black hair and pale gray skin. His suit is black snakeskin. He stands in front of a dozen microphones, clears his throat and says:

"Ladies and gentlemen, I regret to inform you that tragedy has befallen Huntsman City. A man named Leroy White had been working for the Association for a number of years on the Davinson project. However, he decided to take action—against the will of the Association—to find and use the Jabberhouse to rebuild cities bigger and better than they are now.

"His employment has been terminated and the Davinson project has been temporarily placed on hold. We have also put out arrest warrants for known accomplices Imogen Ward and Francesca Collins, who were last seen heading north toward Orbweaver territory. They are to be considered armed and dangerous, and should be reported to the authorities immediately if seen. Another accomplice has been found deceased in the remains of the Jabberhouse, but has not yet been identified.

"We also believe the architects may have been involved in this attack on Huntsman City, but it is currently pending further investigation. We are at present very busy preparing a memorial service for those people and houses lost in the tragic event, and in ensuring our remaining citizens have shelter over their heads while the city is rebuilt. We, at the Association, pray for the safety and continued support of our people, and we mourn for the loss of so many good men and women. I promise that this day shall not soon be forgotten, and that those responsible shall be brought to justice. I believe that this tragedy will only bring us closer together and make us stronger. We will rebuild."

S.T. Cartledge was born and raised in Esperance, Western Australia. He lives in Perth, Western Australia. He graduated Curtin University in 2012 with a Bachelor of Arts (Humanities), with a double major in Creative Writing and Literary & Cultural Studies. He is currently completing his creative writing honours thesis on Bizarro Gothic fiction and experimenting with the Cyberpunk Fantasy genre. He has never worked in a fast-food franchise despite having the necessary qualifications.

BIZARRO BOOKS

CATALOG   SPRING 2012

**ERASERHEAD
PRESS**

Your major resource for the bizarro fiction genre:

WWW.BIZARROCENTRAL.COM

Introduce yourselves to the bizarro fiction genre and all of its authors with the Bizarro Starter Kit series. Each volume features short novels and short stories by ten of the leading bizarro authors, designed to give you a perfect sampling of the genre for only $10.

BB-0X1
"The Bizarro Starter Kit" (Orange)
Featuring D. Harlan Wilson, Carlton Mellick III, Jeremy Robert Johnson, Kevin L Donihe, Gina Ranalli, Andre Duza, Vincent W. Sakowski, Steve Beard, John Edward Lawson, and Bruce Taylor. **236 pages $10**

BB-0X2
"The Bizarro Starter Kit" (Blue)
Featuring Ray Fracalossy, Jeremy C. Shipp, Jordan Krall, Mykle Hansen, Andersen Prunty, Eckhard Gerdes, Bradley Sands, Steve Aylett, Christian TeBordo, and Tony Rauch. **244 pages $10**

BB-0X2
"The Bizarro Starter Kit" (Purple)
Featuring Russell Edson, Athena Villaverde, David Agranoff, Matthew Revert, Andrew Goldfarb, Jeff Burk, Garrett Cook, Kris Saknussemm, Cody Goodfellow, and Cameron Pierce **264 pages $10**

BB-001 **"The Kafka Effekt" D. Harlan Wilson** — A collection of forty-four irreal short stories loosely written in the vein of Franz Kafka, with more than a pinch of William S. Burroughs sprinkled on top. **211 pages $14**

BB-002 **"Satan Burger" Carlton Mellick III** — The cult novel that put Carlton Mellick III on the map ... Six punks get jobs at a fast food restaurant owned by the devil in a city violently overpopulated by surreal alien cultures. **236 pages $14**

BB-003 **"Some Things Are Better Left Unplugged" Vincent Sakwoski** — Join The Man and his Nemesis, the obese tabby, for a nightmare roller coaster ride into this postmodern fantasy. **152 pages $10**

BB-004 **"Shall We Gather At the Garden?" Kevin L Donihe** — Donihe's Debut novel. Midgets take over the world, The Church of Lionel Richie vs. The Church of the Byrds, plant porn and more! **244 pages $14**

BB-005 **"Razor Wire Pubic Hair" Carlton Mellick III** — A genderless humandildo is purchased by a razor dominatrix and brought into her nightmarish world of bizarre sex and mutilation. **176 pages $11**

BB-006 **"Stranger on the Loose" D. Harlan Wilson** — The fiction of Wilson's 2nd collection is planted in the soil of normalcy, but what grows out of that soil is a dark, witty, otherworldly jungle... **228 pages $14**

BB-007 **"The Baby Jesus Butt Plug" Carlton Mellick III** — Using clones of the Baby Jesus for anal sex will be the hip sex fetish of the future. **92 pages $10**

BB-008 **"Fishyfleshed" Carlton Mellick III** — The world of the past is an illogical flatland lacking in dimension and color, a sick-scape of crispy squid people wandering the desert for no apparent reason. **260 pages $14**

BB-009 **"Dead Bitch Army" Andre Duza** — Step into a world filled with racist teenagers, cannibals, 100 warped Uncle Sams, automobiles with razor-sharp teeth, living graffiti, and a pissed-off zombie bitch out for revenge. **344 pages $16**

BB-010 **"The Menstruating Mall" Carlton Mellick III** — "The Breakfast Club meets Chopping Mall as directed by David Lynch." - Brian Keene **212 pages $12**

BB-011 **"Angel Dust Apocalypse" Jeremy Robert Johnson** — Meth-heads, man-made monsters, and murderous Neo-Nazis. "Seriously amazing short stories..." - Chuck Palahniuk, author of Fight Club **184 pages $11**

BB-012 **"Ocean of Lard" Kevin L Donihe / Carlton Mellick III** — A parody of those old Choose Your Own Adventure kid's books about some very odd pirates sailing on a sea made of animal fat. **176 pages $12**

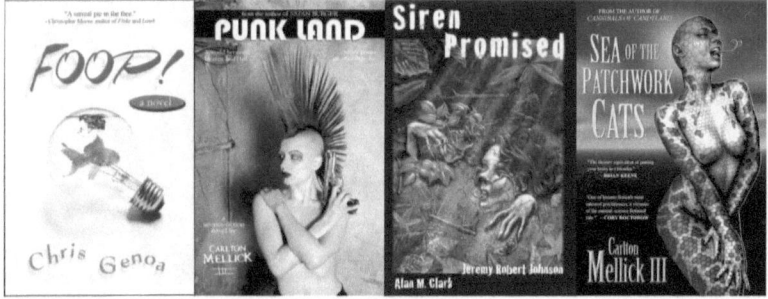

BB-015 **"Foop!" Chris Genoa** — Strange happenings are going on at Dactyl, Inc, the world's first and only time travel tourism company. "A surreal pie in the face!" - Christopher Moore **300 pages $14**

BB-020 **"Punk Land" Carlton Mellick III** — In the punk version of Heaven, the anarchist utopia is threatened by corporate fascism and only Goblin, Mortician's sperm, and a blue-mohawked female assassin named Shark Girl can stop them. **284 pages $15**

BB-027 **"Siren Promised" Jeremy Robert Johnson & Alan M Clark** — Nominated for the Bram Stoker Award. A potent mix of bad drugs, bad dreams, brutal bad guys, and surreal/incredible art by Alan M. Clark. **190 pages $13**

BB-031**"Sea of the Patchwork Cats" Carlton Mellick III** — A quiet dreamlike tale set in the ashes of the human race. For Mellick enthusiasts who also adore The Twilight Zone. **112 pages $10**

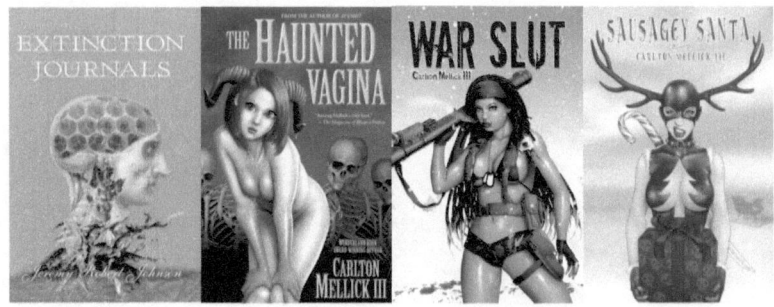

BB-032 **"Extinction Journals" Jeremy Robert Johnson** — An uncanny voyage across a newly nuclear America where one man must confront the problems associated with loneliness, insane dieties, radiation, love, and an ever-evolving cockroach suit with a mind of its own. **104 pages $10**

BB-037 **"The Haunted Vagina" Carlton Mellick III** — It's difficult to love a woman whose vagina is a gateway to the world of the dead. **132 pages $10**

BB-043 **"War Slut" Carlton Mellick III** — Part "1984," part "Waiting for Godot," and part action horror video game adaptation of John Carpenter's "The Thing." **116 pages $10**

BB-047 **"Sausagey Santa" Carlton Mellick III** — A bizarro Christmas tale featuring Santa as a piratey mutant with a body made of sausages. 124 pages $10

BB-048 **"Misadventures in a Thumbnail Universe" Vincent Sakowski** — Dive deep into the surreal and satirical realms of neo-classical Blender Fiction, filled with television shoes and flesh-filled skies. **120 pages $10**

BB-053 **"Ballad of a Slow Poisoner" Andrew Goldfarb** — Millford Mutterwurst sat down on a Tuesday to take his afternoon tea, and made the unpleasant discovery that his elbows were becoming flatter. **128 pages $10**

BB-055 **"Help! A Bear is Eating Me" Mykle Hansen** — The bizarro, heartwarming, magical tale of poor planning, hubris and severe blood loss... **150 pages $11**

BB-056 **"Piecemeal June" Jordan Krall** — A man falls in love with a living sex doll, but with love comes danger when her creator comes after her with crab-squid assassins. **90 pages $9**

BB-058 **"The Overwhelming Urge" Andersen Prunty** — A collection of bizarro tales by Andersen Prunty. **150 pages $11**

BB-059 **"Adolf in Wonderland" Carlton Mellick III** — A dreamlike adventure that takes a young descendant of Adolf Hitler's design and sends him down the rabbit hole into a world of imperfection and disorder. **180 pages $11**

BB-061 **"Ultra Fuckers" Carlton Mellick III** — Absurdist suburban horror about a couple who enter an upper middle class gated community but can't find their way out. **108 pages $9**

BB-062 **"House of Houses" Kevin L. Donihe** — An odd man wants to marry his house. Unfortunately, all of the houses in the world collapse at the same time in the Great House Holocaust. Now he must travel to House Heaven to find his departed fiancee. **172 pages $11**

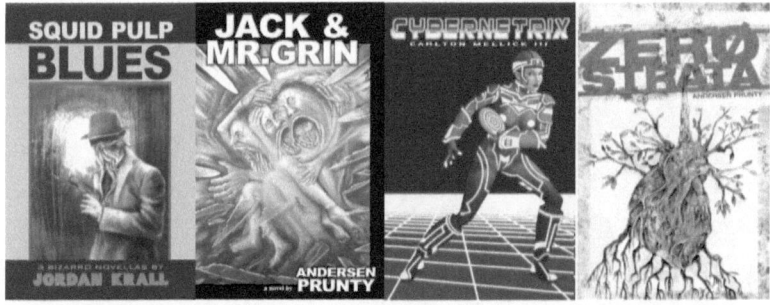

BB-064 **"Squid Pulp Blues" Jordan Krall** — In these three bizarro-noir novellas, the reader is thrown into a world of murderers, drugs made from squid parts, deformed gun-toting veterans, and a mischievous apocalyptic donkey. **204 pages $12**

BB-065 **"Jack and Mr. Grin" Andersen Prunty** — "When Mr. Grin calls you can hear a smile in his voice. Not a warm and friendly smile, but the kind that seizes your spine in fear. You don't need to pay your phone bill to hear it. That smile is in every line of Prunty's prose." - Tom Bradley. **208 pages $12**

BB-066 **"Cybernetrix" Carlton Mellick III** — What would you do if your normal everyday world was slowly mutating into the video game world from Tron? **212 pages $12**

BB-072 **"Zerostrata" Andersen Prunty** — Hansel Nothing lives in a tree house, suffers from memory loss, has a very eccentric family, and falls in love with a woman who runs naked through the woods every night. **144 pages $11**

BB-073 **"The Egg Man" Carlton Mellick III** — It is a world where humans reproduce like insects. Children are the property of corporations, and having an enormous ten-foot brain implanted into your skull is a grotesque sexual fetish. Mellick's industrial urban dystopia is one of his darkest and grittiest to date. **184 pages $11**

BB-074 **"Shark Hunting in Paradise Garden" Cameron Pierce** — A group of strange humanoid religious fanatics travel back in time to the Garden of Eden to discover it is invested with hundreds of giant flying maneating sharks. **150 pages $10**

BB-075 **"Apeshit" Carlton Mellick III** - Friday the 13th meets Visitor Q. Six hipster teens go to a cabin in the woods inhabited by a deformed killer. An incredibly fucked-up parody of B-horror movies with a bizarro slant. **192 pages $12**

BB-076 **"Fuckers of Everything on the Crazy Shitting Planet of the Vomit At mosphere" Mykle Hansen** - Three bizarro satires. Monster Cocks, Journey to the Center of Agnes Cuddlebottom, and Crazy Shitting Planet. **228 pages $12**

BB-077 **"The Kissing Bug" Daniel Scott Buck** — In the tradition of Roald Dahl, Tim Burton, and Edward Gorey, comes this bizarro anti-war children's story about a bohemian conenose kissing bug who falls in love with a human woman. **116 pages $10**

BB-078 **"MachoPoni" Lotus Rose** — It's My Little Pony... *Bizarro* style! A long time ago Poniworld was split in two. On one side of the Jagged Line is the Pastel Kingdom, a magical land of music, parties, and positivity. On the other side of the Jagged Line is Dark Kingdom inhabited by an army of undead ponies. **148 pages $11**

BB-079 **"The Faggiest Vampire" Carlton Mellick III** — A Roald Dahl-esque children's story about two faggy vampires who partake in a mustache competition to find out which one is truly the faggiest. **104 pages $10**

BB-080 **"Sky Tongues" Gina Ranalli** — The autobiography of Sky Tongues, the biracial hermaphrodite actress with tongues for fingers. Follow her strange life story as she rises from freak to fame. **204 pages $12**

BB-081 **"Washer Mouth" Kevin L. Donihe** - A washing machine becomes human and pursues his dream of meeting his favorite soap opera star. **244 pages $11**

BB-082 **"Shatnerquake" Jeff Burk** - All of the characters ever played by William Shatner are suddenly sucked into our world. Their mission: hunt down and destroy the real William Shatner. **100 pages $10**

BB-083 **"The Cannibals of Candyland" Carlton Mellick III** - There exists a race of cannibals that are made of candy. They live in an underground world made out of candy. One man has dedicated his life to killing them all. **170 pages $11**

BB-084 **"Slub Glub in the Weird World of the Weeping Willows"**
Andrew Goldfarb - The charming tale of a blue glob named Slub Glub who helps the weeping willows whose tears are flooding the earth. There are also hyenas, ghosts, and a voodoo priest **100 pages $10**

BB-085 **"Super Fetus" Adam Pepper** - Try to abort this fetus and he'll kick your ass! **104 pages $10**

BB-086 **"Fistful of Feet" Jordan Krall** - A bizarro tribute to spaghetti westerns, featuring Cthulhu-worshipping Indians, a woman with four feet, a crazed gunman who is obsessed with sucking on candy, Syphilis-ridden mutants, sexually transmitted tattoos, and a house devoted to the freakiest fetishes. **228 pages $12**

BB-087 **"Ass Goblins of Auschwitz" Cameron Pierce** - It's Monty Python meets Nazi exploitation in a surreal nightmare as can only be imagined by Bizarro author Cameron Pierce. **104 pages $10**

BB-088 **"Silent Weapons for Quiet Wars" Cody Goodfellow** - "This is high-end psychological surrealist horror meets bottom-feeding low-life crime in a techno-thrilling science fiction world full of Lovecraft and magic..." -John Skipp **212 pages $12**

BB-089 "Warrior Wolf Women of the Wasteland" Carlton Mellick III
— Road Warrior Werewolves versus McDonaldland Mutants...post-apocalyptic fiction has never been quite like this. **316 pages \$13**

BB-091 "Super Giant Monster Time" Jeff Burk — A tribute to choose your own adventures and Godzilla movies. Will you escape the giant monsters that are rampaging the fuck out of your city and shit? Or will you join the mob of alien-controlled punk rockers causing chaos in the streets? What happens next depends on you. **188 pages \$12**

BB-092 "Perfect Union" Cody Goodfellow — "Cronenberg's THE FLY on a grand scale: human/insect gene-spliced body horror, where the human hive politics are as shocking as the gore." -John Skipp. **272 pages \$13**

BB-093 "Sunset with a Beard" Carlton Mellick III — 14 stories of surreal science fiction. **200 pages \$12**

BB-094 "My Fake War" Andersen Prunty — The absurd tale of an unlikely soldier forced to fight a war that, quite possibly, does not exist. It's Rambo meets Waiting for Godot in this subversive satire of American values and the scope of the human imagination. **128 pages \$11**

BB-095 "Lost in Cat Brain Land" Cameron Pierce — Sad stories from a surreal world. A fascist mustache, the ghost of Franz Kafka, a desert inside a dead cat. Primordial entities mourn the death of their child. The desperate serve tea to mysterious creatures. A hopeless romantic falls in love with a pterodactyl. And much more. **152 pages \$11**

BB-096 "The Kobold Wizard's Dildo of Enlightenment +2" Carlton Mellick III — A Dungeons and Dragons parody about a group of people who learn they are only made up characters in an AD&D campaign and must find a way to resist their nerdy teenaged players and retarded dungeon master in order to survive. 232 **pages \$12**

BB-098 "A Hundred Horrible Sorrows of Ogner Stump" Andrew Goldfarb — Goldfarb's acclaimed comic series. A magical and weird journey into the horrors of everyday life. **164 pages \$11**

BB-099 **"Pickled Apocalypse of Pancake Island" Cameron Pierce**—A demented fairy tale about a pickle, a pancake, and the apocalypse. **102 pages $8**

BB-100 **"Slag Attack" Andersen Prunty**— Slag Attack features four visceral, noir stories about the living, crawling apocalypse.A slag is what survivors are calling the slug-like maggots raining from the sky, burrowing inside people, and hollowing out their flesh and their sanity. **148 pages $11**

BB-101 **"Slaughterhouse High" Robert Devereaux**—A place where schools are built with secret passageways, rebellious teens get zippers installed in their mouths and genitals, and once a year, on that special night, one couple is slaughtered and the bits of their bodies are kept as souvenirs. **304 pages $13**

BB-102 **"The Emerald Burrito of Oz" John Skipp & Marc Levinthal** —OZ IS REAL! Magic is real! The gate is really in Kansas! And America is finally allowing Earth tourists to visit this weird-ass, mysterious land. But when Gene of Los Angeles heads off for summer vacation in the Emerald City, little does he know that a war is brewing...a war that could destroy both worlds. **280 pages $13**

BB-103 **"The Vegan Revolution... with Zombies" David Agranoff** — When there's no more meat in hell, the vegans will walk the earth. **160 pages $11**

BB-104 **"The Flappy Parts" Kevin L Donihe**—Poems about bunnies, LSD, and police abuse. You know, things that matter. 132 **pages $11**

BB-105 **"Sorry I Ruined Your Orgy" Bradley Sands**—Bizarro humorist Bradley Sands returns with one of the strangest, most hilarious collections of the year. **130 pages $11**

BB-106 **"Mr. Magic Realism" Bruce Taylor**—Like Golden Age science fiction comics written by Freud, *Mr. Magic Realism* is a strange, insightful adventure that spans the furthest reaches of the galaxy, exploring the hidden caverns in the hearts and minds of men, women, aliens, and biomechanical cats. **152 pages $11**

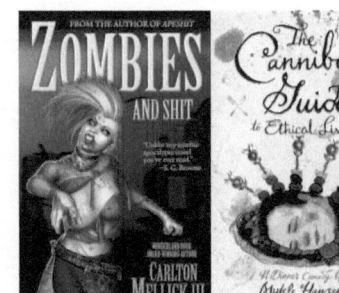

BB-107 **"Zombies and Shit" Carlton Mellick III**—"Battle Royale" meets "Return of the Living Dead." Mellick's bizarro tribute to the zombie genre. **308 pages $13**

BB-108 **"The Cannibal's Guide to Ethical Living" Mykle Hansen**— Over a five star French meal of fine wine, organic vegetables and human flesh, a lunatic delivers a witty, chilling, disturbingly sane argument in favor of eating the rich.. **184 pages $11**

BB-109 **"Starfish Girl" Athena Villaverde**—In a post-apocalyptic underwater dome society, a girl with a starfish growing from her head and an assassin with sea anenome hair are on the run from a gang of mutant fish men. **160 pages $11**

BB-110 **"Lick Your Neighbor" Chris Genoa**—Mutant ninjas, a talking whale, kung fu masters, maniacal pilgrims, and an alcoholic clown populate Chris Genoa's surreal, darkly comical and unnerving reimagining of the first Thanksgiving. **303 pages $13**

BB-111 **"Night of the Assholes" Kevin L. Donihe**—A plague of assholes is infecting the countryside. Normal everyday people are transforming into jerks, snobs, dicks, and douchebags. And they all have only one purpose: to make your life a living hell.. **192 pages $11**

BB-112 **"Jimmy Plush, Teddy Bear Detective" Garrett Cook**—Hardboiled cases of a private detective trapped within a teddy bear body. **180 pages $11**

BB-113 **"The Deadheart Shelters" Forrest Armstrong**—The hip hop lovechild of William Burroughs and Dali... **144 pages $11**

BB-114 **"Eyeballs Growing All Over Me... Again" Tony Raugh**— Absurd, surreal, playful, dream-like, whimsical, and a lot of fun to read. **144 pages $11**

BB-115 **"Whargoul" Dave Brockie** — From the killing grounds of Stalingrad to the death camps of the holocaust. From torture chambers in Iraq to race riots in the United States, the Whargoul was there, killing and raping. **244 pages $12**

BB-116 **"By the Time We Leave Here, We'll Be Friends" J. David Osborne** — A David Lynchian nightmare set in a Russian gulag, where its prisoners, guards, traitors, soldiers, lovers, and demons fight for survival and their own rapidly deteriorating humanity. **168 pages $11**

BB-117 **"Christmas on Crack" edited by Carlton Mellick III** — Perverted Christmas Tales for the whole family! . . . as long as every member of your family is over the age of 18. **168 pages $11**

BB-118 **"Crab Town" Carlton Mellick III** — Radiation fetishists, balloon people, mutant crabs, sail-bike road warriors, and a love affair between a woman and an H-Bomb. This is one mean asshole of a city. Welcome to Crab Town. **100 pages $8**

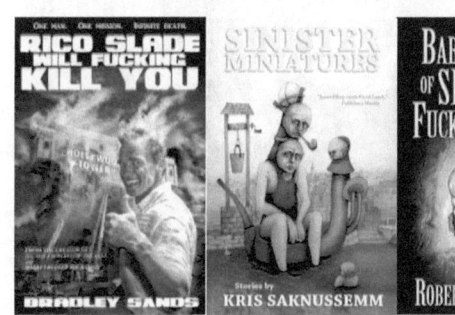

BB-119 **"Rico Slade Will Fucking Kill You" Bradley Sands** — Rico Slade is an action hero. Rico Slade can rip out a throat with his bare hands. Rico Slade's favorite food is the honey-roasted peanut. Rico Slade will fucking kill everyone. A novel. **122 pages $8**

BB-120 **"Sinister Miniatures" Kris Saknussemm** — The definitive collection of short fiction by Kris Saknussemm, confirming that he is one of the best, most daring writers of the weird to emerge in the twenty-first century. **180 pages $11**

BB-121 **"Baby's First Book of Seriously Fucked up Shit" Robert Devereaux** — Ten stories of the strange, the gross, and the just plain fucked up from one of the most original voices in horror. **176 pages $11**

BB-122 **"The Morbidly Obese Ninja" Carlton Mellick III** — These days, if you want to run a successful company . . . you're going to need a lot of ninjas. **92 pages $8**

BB-123 **"Abortion Arcade" Cameron Pierce** — An intoxicating blend of body horror and midnight movie madness, reminiscent of early David Lynch and the splatterpunks at their most sublime. **172 pages $11**

BB-124 **"Black Hole Blues" Patrick Wensink** — A hilarious double helix of country music and physics. **196 pages $11**

BB-125 **"Barbarian Beast Bitches of the Badlands" Carlton Mellick III** — Three prequels and sequels to *Warrior Wolf Women of the Wasteland*. **284 pages $13**

BB-126 **"The Traveling Dildo Salesman" Kevin L. Donihe** — A nightmare comedy about destiny, faith, and sex toys. Also featuring Donihe's most lurid and infamous short stories: *Milky Agitation, Two-Way Santa, The Helen Mower, Living Room Zombies*, and *Revenge of the Living Masturbation Rag.* **108 pages $8**

BB-127 **"Metamorphosis Blues" Bruce Taylor** — Enter a land of love beasts, intergalactic cowboys, and rock 'n roll. A land where Sears Catalogs are doorways to insanity and men keep mysterious black boxes. Welcome to the monstrous mind of Mr. Magic Realism. **136 pages $11**

BB-128 **"The Driver's Guide to Hitting Pedestrians" Andersen Prunty** — A pocket guide to the twenty-three most painful things in life, written by the most well-adjusted man in the universe. **108 pages $8**

BB-129 **"Island of the Super People" Kevin Shamel** — Four students and their anthropology professor journey to a remote island to study its indigenous population. But this is no ordinary native culture. They're super heroes and villains with flesh costumes and outlandish abilities like self-detonation, musical eyelashes, and microwave hands. **194 pages $11**

BB-130 **"Fantastic Orgy" Carlton Mellick III** — Shark Sex, mutant cats, and strange sexually transmitted diseases. Featuring the stories: *Candy-coated, Ear Cat, Fantastic Orgy, City Hobgoblins*, and *Porno in August.* **136 pages $9**

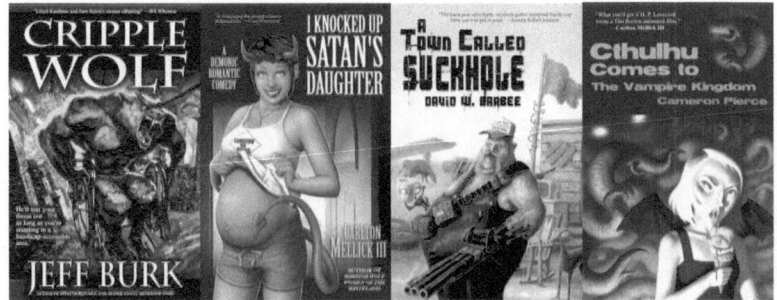

BB-131 **"Cripple Wolf" Jeff Burk** — Part man. Part wolf. 100% crippled. Also including *Punk Rock Nursing Home, Adrift with Space Badgers, Cook for Your Life, Just Another Day in the Park, Frosty and the Full Monty,* and *House of Cats.* **152 pages $10**

BB-132 **"I Knocked Up Satan's Daughter" Carlton Mellick III** — An adorable, violent, fantastical love story. A romantic comedy for the bizarro fiction reader. **152 pages $10**

BB-133 **"A Town Called Suckhole" David W. Barbee** — Far into the future, in the nuclear bowels of post-apocalyptic Dixie, there is a town. A town of derelict mobile homes, ancient junk, and mutant wildlife. A town of slack jawed rednecks who bask in the splendors of moonshine and mud boggin'. A town dedicated to the bloody and demented legacy of the Old South. A town called Suckhole. **144 pages $10**

BB-134 **"Cthulhu Comes to the Vampire Kingdom" Cameron Pierce** — What you'd get if H. P. Lovecraft wrote a Tim Burton animated film. **148 pages $11**

BB-135 **"I am Genghis Cum" Violet LeVoit** — From the savage Arctic tundra to post-partum mutations to your missing daughter's unmarked grave, join visionary madwoman Violet LeVoit in this non-stop eight-story onslaught of full-tilt Bizarro punk lit thrills. **124 pages $9**

BB-136 **"Haunt" Laura Lee Bahr** — A tripping-balls Los Angeles noir, where a mysterious dame drags you through a time-warping Bizarro hall of mirrors. **316 pages $13**

BB-137 **"Amazing Stories of the Flying Spaghetti Monster" edited by Cameron Pierce** — Like an all-spaghetti evening of Adult Swim, the Flying Spaghetti Monster will show you the many realms of His Noodly Appendage. Learn of those who worship him and the lives he touches in distant, mysterious ways. **228 pages $12**

BB-138 **"Wave of Mutilation" Douglas Lain** — A dream-pop exploration of modern architecture and the American identity, *Wave of Mutilation* is a Zen finger trap for the 21st century. **100 pages $8**

BB-139 **"Hooray for Death!" Mykle Hansen** — Famous Author Mykle Hansen draws unconventional humor from deaths tiny and large, and invites you to laugh while you can. **128 pages $10**

BB-140 **"Hypno-hog's Moonshine Monster Jamboree" Andrew Goldfarb** — Hicks, Hogs, Horror! Goldfarb is back with another strange illustrated tale of backwoods weirdness. **120 pages $9**

BB-141 **"Broken Piano For President" Patrick Wensink** — A comic masterpiece about the fast food industry, booze, and the necessity to choose happiness over work and security. **372 pages $15**

BB-142 **"Please Do Not Shoot Me in the Face" Bradley Sands** — A novel in three parts, *Please Do Not Shoot Me in the Face: A Novel*, is the story of one boy detective, the worst ninja in the world, and the great American fast food wars. It is a novel of loss, destruction, and--incredibly--genuine hope. **224 pages $12**

BB-143 **"Santa Steps Out" Robert Devereaux** — Sex, Death, and Santa Claus ... The ultimate erotic Christmas story is back. **294 pages $13**

BB-144 **"Santa Conquers the Homophobes" Robert Devereaux** — "I wish I could hope to ever attain one-thousandth the perversity of Robert Devereaux's toenail clippings." - Poppy Z. Brite **316 pages $13**

BB-145 **"We Live Inside You" Jeremy Robert Johnson** — "Jeremy Robert Johnson is dancing to a way different drummer. He loves language, he loves the edge, and he loves us people. These stories have range and style and wit. This is entertainment... and literature."- Jack Ketchum **188 pages $11**

BB-146 **"Clockwork Girl" Athena Villaverde** — Urban fairy tales for the weird girl in all of us. Like a combination of Francesca Lia Block, Charles de Lint, Kathe Koja, Tim Burton, and Hayao Miyazaki, her stories are cute, kinky, edgy, magical, provocative, and strange, full of poetic imagery and vicious sexuality. **160 pages $10**

BB-147 **"Armadillo Fists" Carlton Mellick III** — A weird-as-hell gangster story set in a world where people drive giant mechanical dinosaurs instead of cars. **168 pages $11**

BB-148 **"Gargoyle Girls of Spider Island" Cameron Pierce** — Four college seniors venture out into open waters for the tropical party weekend of a lifetime. Instead of a teenage sex fantasy, they find themselves in a nightmare of pirates, sharks, and sex-crazed monsters. **100 pages $8**

BB-149 **"The Handsome Squirm" by Carlton Mellick III** — Like Franz Kafka's *The Trial* meets an erotic body horror version of *The Blob*. **158 pages $11**

BB-150 **"Tentacle Death Trip" Jordan Krall** — It's *Death Race 2000* meets H. P. Lovecraft in bizarro author Jordan Krall's best and most suspenseful work to date. **224 pages $12**

BB-151 **"The Obese" Nick Antosca** — Like Alfred Hitchcock's *The Birds*... but with obese people. **108 pages $10**

BB-152 **"All-Monster Action!" Cody Goodfellow** — The world gave him a blank check and a demand: Create giant monsters to fight our wars. But Dr. Otaku was not satisfied with mere chaos and mass destruction.... **216 pages $12**

BB-153 **"Ugly Heaven" Carlton Mellick III** — Heaven is no longer a paradise. It was once a blissful utopia full of wonders far beyond human comprehension. But the afterlife is now in ruins. It has become an ugly, lonely wasteland populated by strange monstrous beasts, masturbating angels, and sad man-like beings wallowing in the remains of the once-great Kingdom of God. **106 pages $8**

BB-154 **"Space Walrus" Kevin L. Donihe** — Walter is supposed to go where no walrus has ever gone before, but all this astronaut walrus really wants is to take it easy on the intense training, escape the chimpanzee bullies, and win the love of his human trainer Dr. Stephanie. **160 pages $11**

www.ingramcontent.com/pod-product-compliance
Lightning Source LLC
Chambersburg PA
CBHW020729250626
47155CB00006B/2226